Woven Wishes

Book Four: Whispered Wishes Series

Karen Pokras

Grand Daisy Press

Grand Daisy Press
PO Box 30241
Elkins Park, PA 19027

Publisher's Note: This is a work of fiction. Names, characters, places, and incidents are a product of the author's imagination. Locales and public names are sometimes used for atmospheric purposes. Any resemblance to actual people, living or dead, or to businesses, companies, events, institutions, or locales is completely coincidental.

Edited by Melissa Ringsted of There For You Editing
Cover by Najla Qamber Designs
Models: Courtney Boyett, Sara Beck, and Brittany Weidman
Model Photographer: Casey Boyett
Book Layout ©2013 BookDesignTemplates.com

Woven Wishes/Karen Pokras. -- 1st ed.
ISBN 978-0-9962843-3-2

For more information, please visit
www.karenpokras.com

"There is hope in dreams, imagination, and in the courage of those who wish to make those dreams a reality."

–Jonas Salk

The Whispered Wishes Series

Four Years Later

TESSA

"**The** Stella Russo?" she shrieked.

Nicholas stood with a casual stance, as if mentioning her name were no big deal.

Placing her hands on her hips, Tessa circled him slowly before coming back around to meet his eyes. "The same Stella Russo who won the Academy Award for best actress in 2006 and 2007?"

"And don't forget 2008," Nicholas reminded her. "It may only have been for a supporting role, but she'd be very upset if you forgot about it. You know how these actresses can be."

"But why? How?" Feeling slightly lightheaded, she slid into the chair the props people had forgotten to remove from the stage.

Opening night at the River House Theater was just months away, and her leading lady, Angela Butler, had quit over the weekend without any notice. If what Nicholas was saying was correct, three-time Academy Award winner Ms. Stella Russo was about to be her new star. Tessa took a deep breath. Was he for real? Having a big name star would surely bring in sell-out crowds on a regular basis. It would be just the miracle her financially strapped theater needed.

"I have connections," Nicholas said, his eyes brightening. "Stella and I met years ago at an awards ceremony after-party, before I knew you. Despite what the tabloids report, she can actually be a nice woman … when she wants to be. We shared dim sum at a place on Sunset Boulevard."

Shaking her head, Tessa looked up at him and smiled. "I keep forgetting you're not a normal guy."

"I'm not quite sure if that's a compliment or an insult," he muttered, furrowing his brow. Walking around the empty stage, he stopped just before reaching the center, the spotlight above casting a glow on him as he looked down at her.

Tessa cocked her head playfully. "In case you haven't noticed, us *normal* people don't have dim sum with Oscar-winning movie stars—or any movie stars for that matter. In fact, I'm not even sure I know what dim sum is."

Nicholas sighed. "As I was saying, when I was in Manhattan on business the other day, I ran into her agent. We were both in between meetings, so we decided to catch up over a glass of scotch. At first he was upset I didn't invite him to the wedding, but you know, we had to draw the line somewhere."

"Five hundred seemed like a good number," Tessa said sarcastically.

"I guess that comes with me not being a *normal* guy? I have a lot of connections. What can I say? It comes with the territory. You love me anyway." He tenderly caressed his wife's face before leaning down to give her a kiss.

"That I do," she replied, wishing the kiss had lasted longer. She loved everything about him and still had to pinch herself regularly to make sure she wasn't dreaming. She couldn't believe how much her life had changed recently. Just a few years ago she was a single mom, struggling to pay her rent, while working for Steven Abbott, the most horrid man who ever existed. At Abbott and Associates, she spent most of her time behind the scenes, compiling accounting reports for an old, stodgy multi-millionaire businessman named Nicholas Schilling, who as it turned out was neither old nor stodgy, although she didn't realize it at the time. She eventually left that job to work at her brother-in-law Ben's plant. Still not her dream job, as the theater had always been her first love, but a huge step up from Abbott and Associates. Now here she was, running a theater and married to Nicholas. Life was good ... very good.

"So, tell me the part where Stella Russo comes in," she coaxed, anxious to get all of the details.

"Well," he continued, putting his hands behind his back as he paced the floor—something her husband tended to do whenever he got excited about new business ventures, "we got to talking about you, your theater, and your dilemma. He made a few phone calls and *Voila!*"

"Nicholas, you know I don't want to use your money to keep this theater afloat," Tessa said, sinking into her seat. While she was appreciative of his enthusiasm, and extremely grateful for her financial security on the home front, she felt uncomfortable asking for anything more. He'd already given her so much.

"Look at me." He grabbed a chair that was off to the side and sat down next to his wife. "Let's get something straight. First of all, we're married now—we have been for almost a year. It's not *my* money, it's *our* money. Second, I know how important this theater is to you. For the past few years, you worked your ass off as the bookkeeper at Ben's plant, saving every penny you could. I know it wasn't easy. And as much as it drove me insane every time you turned down my offer to help you financially, I understood this was something you needed to do by yourself. When this theater went up for sale last year, I let you handle it all on your own. Right down to applying for the loan and getting the funds together for the initial down payment. Having Stella Russo as your new leading lady has nothing to do with money. She offered to come here."

"But I won't be able to even come close to paying her what she's used to receiving. She's a big star. You know our budget for wages is pitiful. That's probably why Angela walked out on us."

"Her agent says she's between projects. Trust me, when it comes to working, a small job is better than no job. This is about timing and opportunity. That's all."

"But—"

"No buts. So what if I used one of my connections? It's time you let me spoil you a little."

Looking over to her husband, Tessa smiled. He was such a good man and sexy as hell. *Pinch.* Yup, still real. "Okay," she smiled, "you win. However, I'm going to be a nervous wreck right up until the moment I meet her … and even after. When do you think that will be by the way?"

"We're having dinner with her tonight, so you two can get to know each other and go over the details."

"Tonight? I'm meeting Stella Russo tonight?" The chair knocked over behind her when she jumped up in a panic. Yes, she needed an actress right away. Hell, she'd needed an actress from the moment Angela quit. But tonight? Stella Russo? She sat back down, this time on Nicholas' lap, feeling lightheaded all over again.

"Don't worry, I'll be right by your side," he said, gently stroking her arm. "It's what I promised at our wedding, remember?" He brought her hand to his lips and tenderly kissed the tips of each finger. "You, my love, just have to remember that you promised to let me be there."

2 AVA

"Thank you so much, Ava. I really appreciate you taking Sophie tonight. My sitter couldn't stay late today. It's a huge help."

"It's no problem," she replied, weariness filling her voice. When didn't Tessa need help? As the oldest sister, Ava felt obligated to look after both of her siblings, but usually she felt more like a mother where her youngest sister was concerned.

Tessa helped Sophie off with her coat and kissed the top of her head.

"Do you really have to go, Mommy?" she asked with the same sad look Ava's own children used on her regularly when they wanted something.

"I'm sorry, sweetie," Tessa replied. "This is a very important dinner. I'll try not to be too late, okay?"

"Logan's in the family room, Soph. Why don't you go see what he's up to?" Ava suggested, trying to make Tessa's departure as painless as possible. They watched as she headed off down the hallway.

"She didn't say good-bye," Tessa said, looking as if she were about to go after her. "I hate it when she's mad at me."

"Don't worry. She's being seven," Ava reminded her, suddenly noticing her younger sister's attire fit for a night on the town: black cocktail dress, heels, hair and makeup perfectly done. *This was her emergency? Must be nice.* Dressing up for Ava meant wearing sweats that didn't have any tears or stains.

Tessa headed toward the door, apparently past her moment of being upset over leaving her daughter. "I'm really sorry for the last minute notice," she began, turning around and taking Ava's hands. "Nicholas set up this business meeting for the theater with this celebrity actress, and ..."

"It's okay, really." She wasn't in the mood to hear the details of her sister's perfect fairy tale life. She had laundry to fold, toys to put away, and dinner to make. Plus, Ryan still needed a ride home from Mrs. Connelly, her babysitter. For two hours, twice a week, she was supposed to be "kid-free" to get stuff done. Somehow it never worked out that way. Today she had extended it to half a day. Hopefully, her three year old wasn't too upset. Glancing at the clock on the wall, she wondered if she could extend it another thirty minutes to five o'clock. Logan still had swim practice to get to. Or maybe she could just drop him off and then get Ryan. After all, her middle child was almost eight, and hardly any of the other parents stayed to watch. Of course, now there was Sophie to worry about as well. Why did she always say yes when Tessa asked for a favor? She assumed it was out of habit.

Before Tessa met Nicholas, Tessa's life as a single parent was so stressful, and Ava knew how difficult being a single parent could be. Sure she was married— her and Max were going on thirteen years now—but if you counted the days he'd actually been home, it had probably been more like five ... maybe six years. Such was the life of an airline pilot's wife. It wasn't easy, and she knew it was even harder for Tessa. Sophie's dad had run out on them, and she'd worked long hours just to make ends meet. Back then she tried to help Tessa as much as she could. She and Holly both did. Yet her youngest sister hadn't been single for a while now, and Ava was *still* doing all these favors for her. Nicholas, of course, had offered to hire a nanny to help, but Tessa would have nothing of it. She had a neighborhood teen come to the house each afternoon so she could work late at the theater, her sisters, and occasionally her parents who lived about an hour away. To her, that was all she needed. As much as

Ava loved her children, she'd have taken that nanny offer any day.

"Thanks, sis, I owe you one. I'll call you later." Tessa swiftly closed the door behind her without looking back or yelling good-bye to Sophie.

You owe me more than one.

"Jenna," Ava called up to the second floor. "Jenna!"

No response. Her daughter was probably listening to music with her headphones on even though she was supposed to be doing homework.

"*Jenna,*" she yelled once more as she walked up the stairs.

Ava opened the door to her daughter's bedroom without a knock, not that her daughter would have been able to hear her anyway.

"Jenna!" she yelled again with an impatient tone, yanking the ear buds out.

"Mom! What are you doing?"

"I've been calling you. I thought I told you no music while you do your homework."

"I'm just taking a little break," she replied.

"A break from what? You just got home from cheerleading practice. The rule is homework first. You know that."

"Fine." She turned toward her book bag, rolling her eyes.

"I saw that."

Ava wondered, as she often did, when exactly her sweet little girl had turned into a pre-teen. According to everyone she talked to, eye rolling came with the territory.

When Ava had Jenna, she'd been so excited to have a little girl … a daughter of her own. Not that she would have been unhappy with a boy, but having grown up as the oldest girl herself, she knew how special that role could be. Once Jenna was born, Ava wanted her to have a sister, so she could experience the same bond she had with her own sisters. However, it seemed she was destined to be the big sister to two younger brothers instead.

"Can you stay with Sophie for a little bit? She's here, and I have to pick up Ryan and take Logan to swim practice."

"Okay, Mom," Jenna said, smiling, obviously trying to get back on her good side.

Despite the occasional tween attitude, Jenna was a good kid. Ava chalked it up to one part raising her daughter correctly and two parts luck.

Ave returned the smile. "Thank you."

Logan didn't seem to mind that his mom wasn't coming inside for swim practice. He'd always appeared to be more independent than Ava remembered Jenna being at that age. She supposed eye rolling from her second child would be coming any day now as well. At least Ryan still enjoyed her company. Ava smiled, thinking about how he climbed into her bed every morning to snuggle. Reminding Logan she'd be back after she picked up his younger brother, she watched as her middle child entered the building. She had a few minutes before she had to go and sat in the parking lot with her head back and eyes closed. Miraculously, it seemed she had everything under control. For the next five minutes at least.

3 HOLLY

olly sat in the doctor's office anxiously waiting for the results, clutching her husband, Ben's hand tightly. She didn't understand why they were having so much difficulty. It seemed unfair. Her older sister had three children she could barely manage, and her younger sister had one she never wanted ... well, she had wanted her, just not so soon. There was no doubt Tessa loved Sophie. They all loved Sophie, and of course Ava could manage her kids just fine. Holly was just feeling bitter. She so wanted a child of her own to love. She'd dreamt of having children for years. It seemed wrong that she and Ben had to work so hard to make that happen. She loved being Aunt Holly, but more than anything wished someone would also call her Mom.

Dr. Rowe closed the door before sitting behind his desk. He opened the manila folder and adjusted his glasses, unable to look Holly and Ben in the eyes.

"I'm sorry," he began.

Holly didn't hear anything the doctor said after that. She and Ben had saved every penny to pay for the in vitro fertilization. She was thrilled when the tests came in positive ... her prayers had finally been answered. As much as she wanted to tell her family the good news, they decided to wait. The doctor had warned them the first trimester could be risky. Seven weeks into the pregnancy, Holly started to bleed. They rushed over to Dr. Rowe's office and had an ultrasound.

She was too numb to cry.

Ben squeezed Holly's hand even tighter, bringing her back to reality.

"If we try again," Ben asked the doctor, "what are the chances?"

"Nothing changes," Dr. Rowe explained. "The risks are the same. We don't always understand why women miscarry. In your case, there's no reason why you shouldn't be able to carry a healthy baby to term. Many couples who miscarry go on to have successful pregnancies."

They sat in silence in the doctor's office as the tears began to stream down Holly's face. Ben stared straight ahead, looking stoic. After a few tortuous moments, Dr. Rowe stood.

"Again, I'm so sorry. I'm afraid I have another patient to see, but please take all of the time you need, and let me know what you decide."

"Thank you, Doctor," Ben said on their behalf.

Making their way through the parking lot toward their cars, Ben tried to tell Holly he would figure out a way to get the money. She knew he was just trying to cheer her up. They'd been through their finances a million times already. The situation was bleak. Ben kissed his wife good-bye and told her not to worry as he got into his car and headed back to work. One day they had a baby, the next day they didn't. Holly couldn't help but wonder why her husband wasn't as shaken up as she was. Why wasn't he there with her to grieve? He had plenty of vacation time accumulated. She needed him ... with her.

She dug her cell phone out of her purse as she walked to her car.

"Hi, it's me. What are you up to?" she asked, holding back another round of tears.

"I'm on my way to pick Ryan up."

"You sound frazzled." Dealing with her sister's problems seemed to be the best way for Holly to ignore her own.

"No. Well maybe a little," Ava laughed. "It's just that Max hasn't been home in days. Then Tessa decided to drop Sophie off without any notice—*as usual*—because she had some glamorous party to go to. Thankfully, I have Jenna to watch her, because Logan has to be picked up in thirty minutes, and Ryan needs to get picked up in between getting Logan. Plus, the house is a disaster, and I have no idea what I'm making for dinner. You know, just a typical day in my fabulous life."

"Why don't you let me get Ryan? I could use a little baby therapy," Holly suggested.

"Don't let him hear you say that. His favorite thing lately is to remind anyone who will listen that an almost four year old is *pwacticawy gwown up.* That kid kills me some times. If I didn't have him around to keep me giggling, I swear, I don't know how I'd stay sane. Some days I wonder why I even had children. My life could be so calm."

Holly's building tears suddenly burst into free flowing sobs.

"Hol, what's wrong? Are you home? Where are you?"

"I'm in the parking lot. Dr. Rowe's parking lot. The IVF didn't hold. I'm not pregnant."

"Oh, honey, I'm so sorry. I really am. I'm a heel ... that was so insensitive of me. I don't know what I was thinking just then. Where's Ben?"

"No, it's not your fault. It's okay. Ben was here, but he left," Holly managed as she tried to catch her breath.

"What do you mean *left?*" Ava asked, concerned.

"No, not like that. He had to go back to work. He told me not to worry. I know he's just trying to be strong for my sake. I really thought … it all feels so final now."

"Don't give up, Hol."

"I feel like we've tried everything within our reach." She held the phone up to her ear with her shoulder while trying to find her car keys.

"You know what Dad would say right about now don't you?" Ava asked.

"Straight up, hold the olives?" Holly knew what was coming.

"No, he'd say …"

"You only fail if you stop trying," they both said together.

Holly wiped her tears and sighed. She knew Ava meant well, but she didn't get it. Not really. She had three kids, which she'd had no problem conceiving. How could she truly understand?

"So, is it okay if I get Ryan?" Holly asked again. "Ben's going to be working late, and I'm not really up for going home to an empty house tonight. Don't worry about dinner. We can order pizza. It's on me."

"Okay, Holly, if that's what you want. Thanks. I'll see you soon."

4 Tessa

Stella snapped her fingers three times before the waiter, an older man who had worked at the restaurant for years, finally made his way over to their table.

"Yes, ma'am?" he asked with a disapproving tone. She might have been accustomed to treating folks like that in Hollywood, but here in Forest Hills, people acted a bit more respectful.

"I ordered medium. This is rare. If I wanted a plate full of bloody meat, I would have asked for it." She pushed the dish toward the waiter, who thankfully caught it before it crashed to the floor.

"I'm so sorry, ma'am," he replied, obviously wanting to say something entirely different to her. "I'll return it to the kitchen at once and have the chef prepare a new filet for you."

"Don't bother. Your establishment is obviously incompetent when it comes to preparing premium steaks. I'll take a Caesar salad instead. I want the Parmesan cheese shaved thin, not shredded or grated, and I want exactly three anchovies and no croutons. Dressing is to be prepared fresh and on the side with a wedge of lemon. Do you think your chef can handle that?"

"Of course, ma'am," he insisted, while looking at Nicholas who mouthed, 'I'm sorry'.

The waiter scurried away, shaking his head.

"Honestly. These small town restaurants are something else, aren't they?" Stella asked, looking directly at Tessa.

"Actually," she said with a forced smile, "this place is one of our favorites. I think you'll be quite pleased with your salad."

Stella Russo might be a big-time star, but that didn't give her the right to be rude. Tessa hoped that attitude of hers didn't carry over onto the stage. If it did, they were going to have major issues. Was Nicholas really friends with this prima donna? Between this and arriving an hour late for dinner, their first business meeting was not getting off to a great start.

After Stella did finally arrive, she spent the first thirty minutes talking non-stop about ... well, herself. She began by describing the most *amazing* role she'd landed on Broadway when she had first started working, followed by her many *amazing* movie roles, and morphed into her sharing a very extensive list of *amazing* leading men she'd *worked* with over the years. All of which were due to her *amazing* talent ... of course. The waiter had to come back three times before she stopped talking long enough to give him her order. Her first order, that is.

"Oh." Stella waved her napkin at Tessa and Nicholas before placing it on her lap. "I'm so sorry. That was a bit harsh. I flew in on the red-eye and am going on forty-eight hours of no sleep. Between that and the limousine driver who apparently had no idea where he was going, my nerves are completely shot. I feel so foolish. When that charming waiter returns, I'll be sure and apologize."

Tessa smiled and nodded. Perhaps she had misjudged Stella. She'd had more than her share of bad days over the years and at times was not always the most polite. It was time to put it all behind them and get to business. "So, Ms. Russo, we're very excited to have you on board," Tessa began, "but I'm afraid we're kind of on a tight schedule. I'm sure Nicholas told you that our former leading lady walked off set in the middle of rehearsals? Opening night is just a few months away."

Stella ignored Tessa and looked only at Nicholas, taking his hands in her own. "Yes. We had a lovely talk about it already, didn't we, darling? You *will* be there during rehearsals, won't you?"

"Oh, um, probably not," Nicholas answered, pulling away to wipe imaginary crumbs off his mouth with his napkin. "I've got my own business to attend to. But I assure you, Tessa is a top-notch director." He looked lovingly over to his wife. "The best actually. Everyone loves working with her. You'll be in very capable hands."

"Well," Stella said, looking first at Tessa, then to Nicholas all the while keeping a sly grin, "I suppose that will do, but I'd rather be in your hands."

Was she serious? No, she hadn't misjudged this woman one bit. She was unbelievable. Tessa watched as Stella moved her arm under the table, shifting her body closer to her husband.

Nicholas suddenly jumped up and back with wide eyes, pushing away what was no doubt an unwanted advance. "Actually, Stella," he said, clearing his throat, "I'm not sure this arrangement is going to work out after all."

"Oh, darling," she exclaimed, placing her arm back on the table, laughing as she took a long sip of her wine. "I'm just playing with you." Stella looked at Tessa with a purposeful stare. "Nicholas and I go *way* back. Anyway, dear, you apparently have a lot to learn about what it means to work with a Hollywood actress.

There's more to it than what's happening on stage. There are also the little extra backstage *perks* I'm entitled to, if you catch my drift. Now, Nick, stop being silly, and sit back down so we can finish discussing the details."

Nicholas caught Tessa's eye as he sat, pulling his chair in and away from Stella. She knew exactly what she needed to do.

"Ms. Russo," Tessa began, her fingers forming tight fists around the napkin on her lap as she tried her best not to lose her temper. If there's one thing she'd learned over the years, it was to not burn bridges, especially with someone as influential as Stella Russo. As much as it killed her, she'd have to swallow her pride on this one. "With all due respect, this is a small town, with a small town theater. I appreciate your offer, but I think Nicholas is right. I don't think this arrangement is going to work."

"You're firing me?" she asked, her voice filling with anger.

"N-no," Tessa told her. "Not at all. I just think with your talent ... your *amazing* talent, this job will only hold you back. It's like you said, you're a Hollywood actress. That's where you belong. On the big stage with a packed house and a giant marquee out front flashing your name." She raised her hands up as if she were picturing such a scene filled with bright lights and fanfare. "As much as we'd love to be able to do that here, we both know it's just not going to happen. Our theater rarely sells out, and we certainly don't have a marquee out front. At most we take out a tiny ad in the local paper. Hell, the salary we'd be paying you would barely cover the cost of this mediocre meal." She looked over to her husband as he smiled and nodded, his face full of pride and approval, giving Tessa the strength she needed to continue. "You're an Academy award-winning actress. Now go find an Academy award-winning role." Tessa stood up, took a deep breath, pointed to the door, and prayed her near Academy award-winning speech would work.

The look on Stella's face was absolutely blank as Tessa quietly slid back into her chair. Had she just hammered the final nail into her tiny theater's coffin? Her heart raced as she waited for Stella to do or say something. *Anything.*

"Well," she finally said, in a surprisingly calm voice, "I believe I do quite agree with you. Having only spent a few short hours here in Forest Hills, I can see this is not the place for me. However, I must say, I'm quite impressed with you, Tessa. For you to sacrifice the success of your theater for my happiness is indeed a noble gesture. One I will not soon forget. I especially appreciate the fact that you're able to recognize my obvious talent. I'll be sure to mention your *little theater* to my publicist upon my return to Hollywood. Perhaps she can work it into her next press release."

Rising from her seat, she kissed Nicholas on both cheeks and whispered in his ear loud enough for Tessa to overhear, "Do look me up the next time you are in town, darling, so we can pick up where we left off." Looking over to Tessa, Stella curtly nodded, before holding her head high and walking off, nearly knocking the waiter over as he carried her Caesar salad toward them on a silver tray.

Tessa held in her laughter until they were sure Stella was safely inside of the waiting limousine.

"What a horrid woman," she said, trying to catch her breath.

"Darling," Nicholas said, trying to imitate her uppity tone, "I will act in your insignificant production, but only if you fly in the best chefs from around the world to prepare all of my meals. However, the food will not be enough to satiate my appetite. You will have to give me your incredibly sexy husband as well."

Tessa looked at Nicholas and smirked. "Very funny, hot shot. A little advance warning would have been nice, you know."

"Honestly, I had no idea she'd act like that. She wasn't that way at all the last time we'd gotten together. I guess a few awards can really change a person."

Sighing, Tessa swirled the water in her glass, watching as the liquid rolled up close to the edge without going over. "And so now I'm once again without an actress ... with only a few months to go and no real budget to hire anyone. What am I going to do, Nicholas?"

Taking his wife's hands, he gazed into her eyes. "You're going to let me help you, that's what."

"I already told you. I don't want your money."

"And I'm not giving it to you."

"Then ... what are you talking about?"

"As I see it, you need money, and I'm looking for a new business venture, so I'd like to invest in the theater." He held up his hand to stop her as she started to speak. "Don't think I'll just be handing over money. In exchange, you will make me your business manager and partner. You handle the creative side, and I handle the financial side. What do you say, Mrs. Schilling? Do we have a deal?"

Tessa studied her husband's face. He seemed sincere. Could this actually work? She didn't really have any other options at this point. She smiled reluctantly and accepted his hand for a shake.

"Deal," she responded.

5 HOLLY

By the time the pizza arrived, Ryan was fast asleep, curled against Holly on Ava's couch. She sat with her nephew for a while, enjoying the serene sounds of his soft and rhythmic breathing, before sliding her arm out carefully from behind his head so as not to wake him. He looked too peaceful to disturb. He could always eat later.

Holly, on the other hand, didn't realize just how hungry she actually was until she'd had some time to relax. As crazy as Ava's house was, it always seemed to calm Holly down. She loved the chaos—there were always kids running, laughing, and even arguing. She loved it all, even the mess; it felt lived in, comfortable.

To her there was nothing better than a house full of children. Her own house was so quiet ... too quiet.

She carefully got up and walked over to the table to grab a slice of the almost gone pizza. Ava's two older children had already devoured it and retreated to fight over whose turn it was to watch television, while Sophie remained at the table, picking at her piece.

"Not hungry, hun?" Ava asked.

"No," Sophie replied, hanging her head down.

Holly sat down next to her niece and rubbed her back. "What's the matter, sweetie? Do you want to talk about it?"

The tears began before she could get the words out. "We were working on a family tree in art class and some kids were teasing me because I don't have a dad."

"What are you talking about? Of course you have a dad. You have Nicholas."

"No, I mean a *real* dad. Mommy said that Scott guy loves me and stuff, but she won't tell me why he's not here."

Holly looked to Ava for help. This was not a discussion they should be having with Sophie, and it wasn't the first time it had come up either. Tessa really needed to be the one talking to her about this; she was old enough to know.

"Oh, honey," Ava said, joining them at the table. "Nobody really knows why your dad isn't here with you, but your mom is right. It doesn't mean he doesn't love you or think about you. It's just ... your dad was so young when you were born."

Holly shut her eyes, willing her thoughts to go away. *They weren't even trying. Sophie was a mistake.* She needed to stop! The circumstances surrounding Sophie's birth were irrelevant. Tessa loved her daughter. They all did. She was just feeling bitter about her own situation.

"You know, in my opinion," Ava continued, "Nicholas is a thousand times more your *real* father than Scott. He loves you so much, Sophie. You're a very lucky girl."

"I know, Aunt Ava. I love Nicholas. He's the one who takes care of me most of the time anyway. Mom's always at the theater, and some days she gets home so late, I don't even see her." She reached for her pizza and took a bite, smiling at her aunts.

Holly gave her niece a kiss on the cheek and walked out into the living room, toward the front door as an overwhelming urge to scream took over her. Ava swiftly followed.

"Hol, I know what you're thinking," she said, grabbing her arm, "but everything Tessa does is for Sophie's best int—"

"I was pregnant," Holly blurted out, interrupting Ava mid-sentence. She didn't know why she'd never bothered to tell either of her sisters before. How were they supposed to support her fully if they never knew? "Seven weeks along ... until today."

Ava wrapped her arms around her. "Honey, I'm so sorry. When you said the in vitro didn't work, I didn't realize you meant— Why didn't you tell me?"

"I don't know," she whispered, wiping away a fresh round of tears. "We were waiting ... and now we have nothing left to wait for. We have nothing at all."

"You know that's not true. You have a lot, and it doesn't mean you won't—"

Holly put her hand up and shook her head to stop Ava. She knew her sister meant well, but she couldn't bear to hear the speech again. *There's still time ... it will happen ... don't give up ... you're still young.* She'd already heard it all. None of it was true.

Ava sighed and gave Holly another hug. "I'm here for you. For whatever you need, Holly. Anything. Are you feeling okay? Any physical pain?"

"Thank you. I'm fine, just a little cramping." Holly sat down on the couch, curled in her sister's arms. "I know I probably surprised you a little there with my announcement, but I kind of don't really want to talk about it right now."

"Okay, hun," Ava said, straightening up.

"So what's going on these days at work?"

Holly laughed, appreciating how Ava was trying to make meaningless conversation to take her mind off her bigger issues.

"Not much. You know how fifth graders can be. The girls look around wondering which boys have a crush on them, while the boys are counting down the minutes until class lets out. Meanwhile, I'm trying to teach them how to solve for "x" so they can all be productive members of society one day. Only eighty-two school days until summer vacation ... not that I'm counting or anything."

At first, Holly and Ben had tried to plan their pregnancy around her work schedule. They'd hoped she would be due at the end of June and able to take the summer off to be with the baby so as not to miss any work. After a while, they realized their plans were not quite so easy to *plan* after all. Eventually, Holly cared less about her due date and more about just getting pregnant.

Ava laughed. Holly knew her sister was counting down the days, too—only she was counting the number of days her kids would still be *in* school. She'd never admit it, but she always seemed thankful for the start of school again in the fall. Holly knew having all three kids home full time for the summer was exhausting. Even so, she'd trade with her big sis any day.

"Any plans for the summer?" Ava asked.

"Ben's boss offered him a couple of weeks at his cabin in the mountains in August. We said no at first because we thought I'd be too far along to travel ... well, I guess we can go now that there's no ba—" Holly stopped herself, unable to finish.

"You should go, Holly!" Ava ordered. Ryan stirred on the other couch, and Ava lowered her voice. "You and Ben deserve a vacation. It sounds perfect. I would love to get away with Max. We haven't been away alone together in years."

"Seriously, with all of the flying Max does, why don't you just go with him? He could fly you to some exotic island—just the two of you. Or to London or Paris! You know how much you've always wanted to go to Paris and see all those art museums you love so much."

"We used to talk about taking a weekend trip to Paris all the time back when Max and I were first dating. That was so long ago. Everything is different now. It's not like I can just get up and go."

"Why not? Ava, you know I'll come watch the kids for you."

"Thanks." She looked like she was going to say more, but the knock at the door interrupted her. "That must be Tessa."

6 TESSA

"What a night!" Tessa and Nicholas burst through the door, laughing hysterically, looking as if they had come from some fancy movie premiere in Hollywood. "Ava, you wouldn't believe it if I told you."

Ryan moaned from the commotion, and while his eyes lightly fluttered, he did not wake up.

"Oh, sorry, I didn't see him there," Tessa said, taking her tone down several notches. "Hey, Hol. I didn't know you'd be here."

Holly smiled politely and pulled the quilt off the back of the couch, carefully wrapping it around Ryan as she picked him up. "I'm going to put him to bed,

Av. In case you were wondering, Tessa, you daughter is upstairs. She fell asleep waiting up for you. *Again*."

"What's with her?" Tessa asked after Holly walked upstairs.

"Oh, she's just having a rough day. Anyway, Sophie's just fine," Ava lied. "So your meeting went well?"

"No, it was awful. Nicholas arranged for Stella Russo to take over as my lead, but it turns out she's an uptight pompous bitch. She left before we ate ... because I fired her. I hope I never see that horrid woman again. Of course, that means I still have no actress for my play."

"Stella ... *Russo*? I don't understand. Why all of the smiles and giggles, then?"

"Your sister's performance was stage-worthy," Nicholas explained. "I mean, it's not every day you see someone put a Hollywood A-lister in their place. It was priceless. Maybe you want to consider taking the lead yourself, Tessa?" he asked, turning to his wife. "You've got some hidden talent there."

"Oh, no," she replied, still laughing. "As much as I actually enjoyed my role tonight, I prefer to be on the sidelines. But that was fun. You should have been there to see the look on her face, Av."

"I'm sure she would have loved to have been there," Holly declared as she came back down the stairs, "but she was too busy having fun wiping your daughter's tears away. Isn't that right, *Av?*"

"I thought you said Sophie was okay?" Tessa asked with a concerned tone. "What's going on?"

"I'll go check on her," offered Nicholas, obviously wanting to get out of the line of fire.

"What's going on is that the poor child misses her mother. She had a bad day at school today. She wanted to talk to you about it, only you weren't around. You're *never* around. She went from her afternoon babysitter, right to her evening caretaker. If I had a child, you'd be damn sure he or she would be my priority."

Tessa just stood there and stared at her sister. Holly's hostility toward her seemed to be getting worse. It wasn't her fault Holly couldn't get pregnant. Of course Sophie was her priority. She may not have been planned, but she loved her more than life itself. Didn't Holly understand the pressure she was under to get this production together—especially without a lead actress? Her daughter knew how much she loved her, didn't she? Didn't she understand her time constraints? Still, a good mother would make time for her daughter. Tessa sank into the living room chair, hanging her head as tears overflowed past her eyes and down her cheeks.

"I'm so sorry, Tessa." Holly rushed over to her to rub her back gently. "I didn't mean it like that. I had a really crappy day."

"I'm sure Tessa understands. It's been a tough day for all of us," Ava said, smiling.

Tessa looked up at her oldest sister. Ava always was the glue. It was rare that she ever made reference to having a bad day herself. Tessa knew her life wasn't easy. She and Max had married so quickly. It was a whirlwind romance straight out of college. They'd only known each other a few weeks before Max proposed. Then Jenna came along before they knew it, and all plans were off the table.

The plan was that while Max was getting his pilot's license, Ava would run some fancy art gallery out west. She'd had big dreams of one day even owning her own gallery. Tessa remembered as a child, Ava would hang all of their artwork in their living room and then advertise her big 'opening night exhibit' for all of the neighbors to come and look. They would, too. She'd serve cookies that they'd all help bake and lemonade Mom had bought from the store. Some of the neighbors even bought the artwork. Seemed Ava had a real flare for arranging and selling their scribbles.

Unfortunately, her pregnancy with Jenna was not an easy one. At six months in, she was put on strict bed rest. The gallery brought in a temporary replacement. After Jenna's birth, Ava continued to work in the gallery, but it was challenging with a baby at home and a husband always on the road, or at least in the sky. Soon after that, Logan was born, and they moved back to Forest Hills. Once back east, she never returned to work in a gallery.

Holly, on the other hand, always dreamed of being a stay-at-home mom with a house full of kids, but had to settle for a classroom full of kids instead. For many years, Tessa's sisters were always the ones picking up her pieces. Now that she had Nicholas, she hoped she could be there more for them, although she felt as if things weren't turning out that way just yet.

Now Tessa was worried about Ava. She knew she'd been stressed out lately with Max gone for such long stretches, but she'd wondered if there was something additional going on. And what about Holly? Was it more than just her usual *still not pregnant* stuff?

"What's the matter with you two?" she asked. "What did I miss?"

Tessa caught Holly shake her head ever so slightly at Ava.

She straightened up in her chair. "Secrets? Since when do the Haines girls keep secrets from each other? Come on, now, spill it."

"Tessa, love," Nicholas walked back into the room with a sleeping Sophie in his arms. "If you want to still visit with your sisters, I can take Sophie home."

"No, that's okay," she said, standing up. "Ava looks tired. I think I'd better leave with you."

"Actually, why don't you stay?" Ava insisted, suddenly cheering up. "It will be fun … like old times. We could use a girls' night. You can sleep in the guest room. I'll take you home in the morning."

"Are you sure?" Tessa asked, wrapping her arms around Sophie. The last thing she wanted was for her daughter to feel like she was deserting her again.

"It's fine," Nicholas replied. "Sophie's asleep, and I'm anxious to get started on the budget for the theater, so I'll just be staring at boring spreadsheets all night."

"Well … okay, but promise you'll call me if she wakes up and wants me to say goodnight, or I can read a story to her over the phone, or sing to her, or—"

"She'll be fine," Nicholas interrupted, smiling. "You can do all of that and more tomorrow, and every night after that—especially now that I'll be able to take some of the pressure off at the theater." Tessa followed her husband out to the car to help him get Sophie comfortable and buckled into the backseat.

"Are you sure?" she asked again.

"Yes." He wrapped his arms around his wife. "Go be with your sisters. I love you."

7 AVA

Tessa sat on the couch and stared out the window while Holly checked on Jenna and Logan upon hearing their banter coming from upstairs. One minute fighting, one minute laughing. Of course, they were both supposed to be getting ready for bed quietly. The bigger concern was that they'd wake their younger brother. Ava wanted to go up herself, but she knew Holly needed to do this. The truth was, out of the three sisters, Holly had always been the best at settling her kids down.

"Are you just going to sit there and mope all night?" Ava asked, shaking out a shirt from the laundry basket that had been sitting on the floor for the past three days. "I thought we were going to have a fun girls' night."

"Folding clothes?" She motioned to the item in her sister's hands. "What you're doing isn't exactly fun."

"True. But it's better than just sitting there stewing." Ava folded the shirt and added it to the small pile of clothes waiting to be put away. "Actually, I was thinking we could have a true girls' night. When was the last time we did something fun like hair and nails?"

"Uh … maybe when we were Jenna's age. Aren't we a little old for that?" Tessa asked, going back to staring out the window.

Ava sat on the couch. Was there anything she could say to make her younger sister feel better about the situation with Sophie? "Tess, you know Holly didn't really mean any of that stuff earlier, right?"

"I guess. It's just that … it's all true. With everything going on at the theater, I haven't been home, and now I feel guilty that I'm here supposedly having fun when I should be home with her."

"So if you sit here and mope will make it better? She's asleep. What were you planning on doing at home, sitting up by her bed all night?"

"At least I'd be there. I feel like a complete failure as a mother."

"Oh, enough already," Holly stated as she came into the room. "I apologized. I honestly didn't mean it." She knelt down next to her sister by the couch and put her hands on her knees. "Look, I'm sorry. It sounds like we all had a crummy day. I think—"

The piercing sound of the phone ringing interrupted Holly from finishing.

"Hold that thought." Ava reached for the phone. "Hello? ... Hi sweetie. She sure is, hold on."

"It's Sophie," Ava said, handing the phone to Tessa.

"Hi, baby. Are you okay? ... Really? ... Ha ha ... I won't tell. I miss you, too ... Do you want me to come home? ... Okay, that sounds like fun ... Yes, I promise. It's a date, and I'll see you in the morning ... Call me if you need anything. I love you." She wiped a tear from her eye and handed Ava the phone.

"So?" Holly asked.

"She said she was wide awake by the time they got home, so Nicholas is letting her watch TV, but she's not supposed to tell me that part, and he also said she can go to school late so she can see me in the morning. Tomorrow night we're going to have a movie marathon. Oh, and she was hungry because she didn't have much for dinner, so Nicholas said she could make a peanut butter and jelly sandwich if she promised to make him one, too." Tessa laughed. "I don't know who spoils who more in that relationship. She sounded ... happy and tired. I'm thinking she'll be asleep in twenty minutes tops."

"So can *we* have some fun now?" Ava asked.

Tessa smiled. "Yes, but first you two need to fill me in on these secrets of yours, and why I'm not the only one who had a bad day. It's time you let me help you for a change. Ava, go grab a bottle from that stash I know you have. I'm calling an official emergency meeting of the **S**ecret **H**aines **O**rder of **E**ndearing **S**isters."

"**SHOES**?" Holly remarked. "We haven't had a SHOES meeting since we were teenagers." She giggled and rubbed her chin. "Remember our last meeting, Ava? We swiped that bottle of vodka from Dad's workbench. He hid it in that old drill case. Well, yours was just water, Tessa. We do have some scruples you know. I wonder why he never ratted us out to Mom."

"Probably because he knew he'd get in as much trouble as we would if Mom found out he was sneaking vodka," Tessa said, laughing. "I can't believe mine was just water. I thought you guys loved me."

"We do," Holly told her. "We may have been crazy, but we weren't stupid enough to give a twelve year old vodka. Ava, you're being awfully quiet. Don't you remember?"

Ava laughed and nodded. Yes, she remembered that meeting well. She was eighteen at the time. Holly was sixteen, and Tessa was barely twelve. As the oldest sister, she'd called the meeting because Holly was upset over some boy. They met in the shed behind the house after dark when their mom and dad were out playing bridge at their Aunt Donna's house. Their parents always stayed out until at least midnight. Ava had lit a bunch of the smelly candles from their mom's bathroom and poured vodka for herself and Holly. They brought a special thermos for Tessa and told her it was vodka infused with special oil imported from India, guaranteed to make her breasts grow. Ava still couldn't believe they'd pulled that one off with a straight face. Then, she called the meeting to order, calmed Holly down, and suddenly, just like that, everything was okay once again in the world of the Haines sisters. Shortly after that, she'd left for college. Despite many heartbreaks and other traumatic events over the years, they hadn't had a SHOES meeting since. They were definitely due.

"It's been ages," Ava said with a knowing smile. "Holly, weren't you all upset about some boy at that meeting? Whatever happened with him?"

"You don't remember?" Holly laughed. "It was Ben! You know ... my husband? He sucked face with that Michelle slut after taking me to the Soph Hop. I was so heartbroken."

"Well, you can't really blame him. High school boys usually go after the sluts," Tessa retorted, teasingly.

"Ugh. What that woman put us through. She's more than just a slut, she's a—"

"Ladies!" Ava yelled, as she heard Jenna and Logan's banter pick up again from the second floor. She brought her voice back down to a whisper. "Can we hold off on the slut talk until the kids are asleep?

Tessa, why don't you go make up the bed in the guest room? Holly, can you help again with Logan and Jenna? I'll set up for the meeting. We'll meet back here in twenty minutes."

8 AVA

"**N**o vodka I'm afraid," Ava said as Tessa re-entered the living room. The space was a bit cozier than the shed they'd sat in years ago. With her sisters busy upstairs, Ava had placed pillows and blankets over the floor. She lit the final candle and walked over to the wine rack to pull out two bottles. "White or red?"

"Both, of course," Tessa stated matter-of-factly. She picked up the toy hammer from Ryan's tool kit that Ava had put out to use as their gavel, and Ava promptly snatched it away.

It was a long-standing tradition for her to lead their SHOES meetings, even if it had been almost twenty years since their last one. The fact that Tessa had called the meeting was irrelevant, she was the one her sisters came to most often whenever there was a problem. Ava often wished *she* had an older sister. Not that she couldn't share her own problems with her younger sisters, she just didn't feel that same level of support that she'd given them. They were always so busy with their own issues. They rarely—if ever— seemed to notice she had problems, too.

Ava's husband, Max, was rarely home. The demands from the airline seemed to increase by the hour. Airline pilots were losing their jobs every day. True, Max was under contract and was a union member, but these days, those things seemed to mean very little. Airlines were struggling. If they went out of business, pilots were out of work—contract or no contract. Max had no choice but to give in to the increased hours. Ava understood, but it didn't make her life any less difficult. In addition to the stress of taking care of three children on her own, there was the growing strain in her marriage. Ava sometimes wondered if Max purposefully chose routes that would keep him out of the house for days at a time. Maybe she was just imagining things.

"Logan gave me a little trouble at first." Holly came into the living room and made herself comfortable on the floor. "He argued that nine-thirty was way too early for any self-respecting seven year old to be going to sleep, but finally gave in when I told him he could come over Saturday to play with the puppy."

"Thanks, Hol," Ava said, handing her sister a glass of wine. "You did pretty good actually. I was expecting way more of a fight."

"Jenna fell asleep the minute she put her earbuds in to listen to music. I think the kids wiped her out tonight."

"I swear, those earbuds are going to become a permanent fixture in her head," Ava muttered, handing Tessa a glass as she made herself comfortable. "One day, I'm going to have to have them surgically removed."

"Now I know why I got *make up the guest bed* duty, and you got *put the kids to bed* duty, Hol." Tessa said, looking a little sad again. "You really are a natural."

"Yeah," Holly replied. "A natural mom to the children I'll never have."

"Not never. It'll happen," Tessa told her. "I have a good feeling about it."

Ava gave Holly a hug. She hated to see her sister in so much pain. She could see the tears starting to form in her eyes. *Damn it, Tessa.* It was an innocent comment, but still.

"What?" Tessa asked. "Is someone going to tell me what's going on? We're all here now. Let's get this meeting started, Ava."

"... and remember that guy who worked at the movie theater over on Singer Street, Hol?" Tessa laughed so hard she could hardly speak. "He had the biggest crush on you. Every time we went in there, his hands shook so much he could barely hand you your popcorn without spilling it. Good thing you never ordered a soda."

Holly giggled. "I always wanted to, but I felt so sorry for the guy. I just knew he'd spill it everywhere. Man, was I thirsty by the time I got home." She grabbed the second bottle of wine and filled her cup. "What was his name? Gene, George, Geoffrey—"

"Gerry!" they all blurted out, then erupted in uncontrollable laughter.

"Ssh, ssh, ssh ... you'll wake the kids," Ava said when she could catch her breath.

The first bottle of wine was long gone, and the second bottle was nearly empty. They'd spent the last hour drinking and reminiscing, but they still hadn't actually discussed the problems at hand. Even so, Ava felt more relaxed than she had in ages.

"Oh crap," Holly said, trying to stand up. "I need to get home. I have to work tomorrow, and Ben's going to be getting home soon." She took a step backwards and stumbled back down onto the pillow.

"I don't think you're going anywhere, sweets," Ava noted. "You can sleep with Tessa in the guest room. I actually swiped your keys while you were upstairs with Logan, and already called Ben at the plant to let him know you'd be staying the night. He told me to tell you he'll take care of calling in sick for you in the morning."

"Always so responsible, even when drunk," replied Holly.

"I'm barely buzzed," Ava said. "For the record, I'm still nursing my second glass. You two lushes pretty much drank both bottles on your own."

Tessa reached over for what was left of the second bottle. "This is going to be painful in the morning." She filled her glass, finishing it off. "Oh well, it's not like I'll be able to get any work done. I have to wait until Nicholas finishes the budget and tells me how much I can spend on a new leading lady. Who do these middle-aged prima donnas think they are anyway? First they screw me, and then they try to screw my husband? They can go fuck themselves."

"Atta girl, Tessa," Holly said. "Fuck 'em. Fuck 'em all and their stupid normal uteruses, too, while you're at it. Fuck 'em for being able to get pregnant and for being able to stay pregnant. That's the trick, you know. Once that little bean gets in there, it has to stick, right? That's hard part. So, I'm with you, Tessa! They can go fuck off!"

"Uh, Hol," Tessa said. "I'm talking about women in their fifties who are probably past their baby-making years. Does this have anything to do with what happened today? I feel like this topic got a bit sidetracked."

Holly looked from Tessa to Ava and burst into tears. Her two sisters rushed to her side. "You tell her, Ava," Holly said. "I can't."

Ava nodded, still cradling Holly. Her own problems seemed so insignificant at the moment. "Holly lost a baby today," Ava explained calmly.

"What?" Tessa asked in shock. "She was pregnant?"

Ava nodded. "Her and Ben did another round of IVF."

"I remember," Tessa said. "I thought we were still waiting for results. Has that much time passed?"

"It's been seven weeks," Ava answered.

"Wow," Tessa replied. "I guess I lost track of time. I'm so sorry, Holly. I didn't realize."

"It's okay, really," Holly said, calming down. "We didn't tell anyone we were expecting. We wanted to wait until after the first trimester. We'd just passed the halfway point. Then, this morning I started bleeding ... a lot."

"Oh my God. I'm so sorry, Hol. But you can try again, right?"

Ava knew this line of questioning would upset her sister, so she decided to answer on her behalf. "The doctors think it's best if they take a break for a while."

"Then you can try, right? I'm sorry, I don't mean to push. I know this must be hard."

"It's okay. It feels good to finally have you know and being here with you two. Plus, the two bottles of wine helped. Sorry your day was on the rough side, too."

Tessa sighed. "So that was the big secret. Well, I love you, you know that. And I'm here for you. We all are. And I'm sorry I'm such an insensitive clod."

Holly hugged her and shook her head. "I love you, too. And you're not. Well, maybe a little, but I am, too, so it's all good," she laughed. "Okay, but now we need to be done talking about it because I prefer to be a happy drunk."

"Got it," Tessa said, wiping her tears away. "And what about you, Ava? Everything going okay with you? What about your crappy day?"

Ava looked at Tessa. She appreciated the concern, but didn't feel right dumping her problems on her younger sisters. They had enough to worry about, and they were drunk. "Oh you know, same old, same old. I wish Max were here more, but otherwise everything is fine. I was just overreacting." *Damn.* Why was it so hard to tell them the truth?

"Okay," Tessa replied. "At least one of us has it together." Tessa raised her glass to toast her older sister.

Ava smiled. *Did she?* she thought to herself.

"We really need to do this more often," Tessa slurred. "You sure you don't have a bottle of vodka hidden away somewhere?"

"We really need to get you and Holly off to bed," Ava corrected.

Tessa raised her glass. "To vodka, and wine, and bed, and to the **S**ecret **H**aines **O**rder of **E**ndearing **S**isters."

The three woman raised their glasses to formally end their meeting and quietly shouted, "To SHOES: Through thick and thin, heels and flats, our secrets stay within. We're not just friends, we're sisters, too. Bound by blood until the end."

9 TESSA

"Mommy! You're back!"

Tessa's headache instantly went away at the sight of her daughter rushing toward her with her arms spread open. Out of the corner of her eye, she watched as her sister pulled out of the driveway. To save Ava the trip, Holly had offered to drive Tessa back on her way home first thing in the morning. The Haines sisters had stayed up way too late, over-indulged in wine, and shared many, many secrets. It had been the perfect night and was long overdue.

"There's my princess," she crooned, scooping her daughter up in her arms. "Boy, did I miss you."

"I missed you, too, Mommy," Sophie replied, nuzzling into the crook of her neck.

"What about me?" Nicholas asked, walking in to the room to greet his wife. "Did anyone miss me?"

"Oh, Nicholas," Sophie giggled. "How could I miss you? You were here the whole night."

"That's right," he told her, tickling her as he kissed Tessa hello.

"Well, I missed you," Tessa said, beaming. Even four years later, her heart fluttered every time her husband walked into the room. "I don't like being away from either one of you." She put Sophie down and smiled wide with adoration at the sight of her family standing before her.

When Sophie's dad, Scott, deserted Tessa while she was still pregnant, she felt as if her life were over. Scared and alone, with a baby on the way, Tessa was grateful for the support of her family. She eventually moved into a tiny rundown apartment, where she struggled to make ends meet as a single mom. As for men, they were the last thing on her mind. Now, here she was—living a dream life with Sophie and the most amazing man she'd ever met.

"Mommy, I picked out three movies for tonight," her daughter began, pulling Tessa out of her thoughts. "The one with the robots who turn evil and try to take over the world, the one about the secret agent with that funny accent, and the one where they try to rescue the girl from the curse of the pirates."

Raising her eyebrows, Tessa looked over to Nicholas, who just smiled and shrugged. "Sophie, sweetie, are you sure those are age appropriate? When did you stop watching movies with cute penguins and princesses in them?"

"Mom, I'm almost eight."

"*Mom*?" Tessa repeated. "A minute ago, I was still *Mommy*. Is this some weird time warp dream or something? And last I checked, almost eight means you're still seven and nowhere near close to the thirteen you need to be in order to watch those PG-13 movies. Now how about *I* pick the movies?"

"Oh, okay," Sophie gave in, looking defeated. "No princesses or penguins."

"Deal," Tessa replied, trying to hold in her laughter.

"It was a good try, sport," Nicholas offered, "but I warned you it probably wouldn't work. You better go get ready for school."

"When did she grow up?" Tessa asked, as she watched her daughter walk up the stairs toward her bedroom.

"She's not grown up." Nicholas draped his arm around her shoulder. "She's only seven and still your little girl. In fact, she'll always be your little girl."

"But when did princesses go away? Princesses used to be all she cared about. Remember?"

"How could I forget?" Nicholas responded, laughing. "If it weren't for Sophie, I'd never know about Princess

Aurora. In fact, I'm pretty sure Her Royal Highness is responsible for us being a family."

Tessa let out a tiny laugh as she nodded her head. It was true. At three years old, Sophie had been obsessed with the beautiful princess from Sleeping Beauty. On the day she met Nicholas for the first time, he surprised her with a magnificent Princess Aurora doll. For Sophie, it was love at first sight ... with both the doll and Nicholas. For Tessa, the fact that this man did something so thoughtful and unnecessary for her daughter only made her love for him, whether she was ready to admit it at that time or not, even stronger.

"Sweetheart? Why are you crying?" Nicholas asked, wiping her tears away.

"We used to be so close, Sophie and me, and now I feel like I've missed the last year of her life. I mean, those movies—I never even knew she was interested in stuff like that. I can never get that time back with her."

"Maybe not," Nicholas said, gently caressing her back, "but you can get to know her now. Come here." Taking Tessa's hand, he led her over to his computer and sat down as she peered over his shoulder. "I want to show you what I've been working on. This is going to free up so much of your time."

Opening up a spreadsheet on the monitor, he started explaining equations and graphs. To anyone else, it might have looked like a bunch of garbled numbers, but Tessa had worked in the accounting field for several years, many of which were spent creating the exact same types of reports. To her, these all made perfect sense, and for the first time since she'd opened her theater, the numbers actually worked. While the budget Nicholas created was modest, it would get Tessa's production up and running. There was enough money to finally make her vision work. First on the agenda would be putting out a casting call for a new leading lady.

As if he could read her mind, Nicholas stated, "I've already put a classified in the online trade magazines. I figured it would be the quickest way to get the word out. Auditions are today at eleven. With this type of streamlining, you'll be able to get everything done during regular working hours."

"You're amazing," she exclaimed, wrapping her arms around her husband's neck from behind. "And ..."

"It's okay," he smirked, "you can say it, I'll only gloat for a week or so."

Rolling her eyes, she continued, "And you were right. I should have accepted your help from the beginning."

"Oh, no, really, go on," Nicholas said, waving his hand in front of his face as if it were nothing. He paused and turned to look at his wife. "No really. Go on."

She pushed him away.

"What's that, Sophie?" he asked, backing out of the room with his hand up to his ear. "You need help with something, also?" He winked at his wife and blew her a kiss as he walked away.

Tessa sat down at the keyboard and looked at the spreadsheet again. All those stressful months, all that time away from Sophie ... it all could have been avoided if she hadn't been so stubborn. Sighing, she closed the document and opened her email: Junk, junk, junk ... What the ... *No ... Please God ... No.*

"Nicholas. NICHOLAS!"

10 HOLLY

Holly walked through her front door still in a daze. There was no doubt hanging out with her sisters last night was a much-needed diversion, but it didn't change the fact her baby was no longer growing inside of her. She closed her eyes, placed her hand across her abdomen, and leaned her head against the wall, as her purse fell to the floor. Would the empty feeling deep within her ever go away? Ben's hand rested gently on top of hers, and her tears once again began to fall.

"What are you doing home, babe?" she finally asked, eyes still closed. "I thought you had the early shift today."

"I took the day off," he answered softly.

His voice sounded shaky, not confident and strong as it usually did. It threw her off, and she lifted her head, meeting his gaze.

His eyes were bloodshot and swollen with bright red rims.

"Are you okay?"

He nodded. "I'm sorry. I shouldn't have left you like that yesterday, in the parking lot. I just didn't know how to ... I didn't know what to ..."

"I know." Pulling him in tight against her, she ran her fingers through the soft waves on the top of his head, mixing in her tears, as he trembled against her. "I know," she whispered again. Hearing his muffled sobs against her neck, she held him even tighter, taking in his scent—the scent that forever brought her comfort, even today.

"We'll get through this, I promise," he said, pulling back slightly. Taking hold of both of Holly's hands, he led her to the couch to sit down. "I know you're worried about finances, but I talked to Nicholas last night. He wants to help. He offered to pay for another round—"

Holly put her hands on her husband's lips to stop him from continuing. "Ben, I don't know if I can go through this again," she told him. "We just lost our baby. I'm an emotional wreck right now."

"Of course, Hol. I didn't mean immediately. We both need some time to heal."

"I don't think you understand. What I mean is it's very generous of Nicholas to offer to help, and you know how much I want to have a family, but I'm beginning to think my body is trying to tell us something. We've spent years going to doctors. I've taken pills, done the injections, had scans and countless other procedures. You've had your share of tests as well. Every procedure that didn't work was disappointing, but it wasn't the end of the world, because we hadn't exhausted all of our options yet. And then, just as we were on our final attempt, a miracle happened. I can't remember ever being happier, can you?"

Ben shook his head no, his eyes filling with tears once more.

"So why? Why would *the powers that be* put us through everything we've been through, all of the heartache and pain, give us the one thing we wanted more than anything else in the world, and then when we're finally happy, take it all away ... just like that? *Why?*"

Holly regarded her husband as he hung his head, unable to look her in the eyes. "I know it doesn't seem fair, but maybe—"

She cut him off. "Maybe we're just not meant to have children of our own. Maybe losing a baby was the only way to get the message across to us."

"You're wrong," he stated, lifting his head. Taking her face in his hands, he stared directly into her eyes.

"You love children. It's what makes you such an amazing teacher. Don't you see, Hol? Even your career path proves you're a nurturing caregiver. You love those kids as if they were your own. That's your sign right there. You were meant to be a mom."

"Or maybe the sign is that the reason I love the kids in my classroom so much is because they're the only ones I'm going to get."

"No," Ben replied assertively, shaking his head. "I don't believe that for a second. And what about me? I still want to be a dad. I don't have a classroom full of kids to fill that need. We were meant to be parents. Our time will come. And there's still adoption."

Tessa smiled at her husband. Adoption wasn't off the table. In fact, she always assumed they'd adopt at some point. However, in her mind she saw it as a way to supplement her family, not as the only means to having a family. She yearned to know what it was like to carry a baby ... to have a living being that she and Ben created together grow inside of her.

"I know it's not what you've dreamed about," he continued, still talking about adopting, "but it's a way for us to be parents if we can't ... You know what I think?"

"What?" she asked. He was so optimistic, no matter what the situation, and they'd been through a lot together. She'd always loved that about her husband. However, her getting pregnant was one thing he couldn't control or fix, neither of them could.

"I think we're putting too much pressure on ourselves. We need a break."

"What do you mean?" She furrowed her brow. Usually when a man told a woman they needed a break, it wasn't good news. Surely he wasn't suggesting they—

Sensing her confusion, he quickly clarified, "I'm talking about getting away ... for a vacation. My boss still has the cabin available. Remember the one he offered us before we knew about the ... Well, we don't have to wait until the summer. We can go over spring break, or take a long weekend. Just the two of us—alone—no work, no phones, no stress. What do you think?"

Curling her body into the crook of Ben's outstretched arm, Holly nodded. It wouldn't solve their problems, of course, but a change of scenery would be good for them. They needed to re-charge and focus on something non-baby related. Was that possible? It had to be for her own sanity.

"Okay," she smiled, "let's do it. Let's go away. Soon. But you have to promise me there will be no baby talk up until or during our vacation. Please?"

"Are you sure that's what you want?" he asked. "You don't even want to talk about ..." He glanced down at her hand, once again resting on her abdomen.

"We can talk about our child whenever you want," Holly said, managing a smile. "I meant I didn't want to talk about getting pregnant ... or possibly adopting.

Not yet. Once we get back, and we're relaxed maybe we can look at our options again. Okay?"

"Okay," Ben said, pulling her in tight.

11 AVA

"I see the laundry elves didn't come while I was out," Ava mumbled as she and Ryan entered the house.

"What, Mama?" he asked with a confused expression on his face.

"Nothing, sweetie. Why don't you go play for a little bit while I put all this away and figure out what we're going to do today?" How she wished she could drop her son off at Mrs. Connelly's for a few hours again. Between the impromptu late night with her sisters, an old dog who decided at four in the morning he suddenly had to get let out, having extra mouths to feed at breakfast, and having to drive Logan and Jenna to school, Ava felt like she'd already put in a full day. At least Holly helped get Tessa home. Now she had stuff to do around the house while entertaining her youngest child who unfortunately gave up napping long ago. *Naps.* What a concept. Ava would gladly take one. Who was the genius that decided naps shouldn't be a forever thing? Unfortunately, her sitter wasn't available today, not that Ava would take him to her anyway. She was still feeling a little guilty over the fact that Ryan had put in extra time there yesterday.

"This laundry is not going to fold itself," she reminded herself out loud, staring at the pile of clothing in hopes that some sort of telekinesis might kick in. Was she imagining things, or had the number of items in the basket increased since last night? She grabbed a sweatshirt off the top and began the arduous task, stacking each piece according to its owner.

Thirty minutes later, she found last weekend's *Forest Hills Times* underneath it all. Collapsing on the couch, she skimmed through the first section, making her way to the only news that really mattered to her: Arts and Entertainment.

"No way," she whispered to herself. "I didn't know that was coming to town." She checked her watch and stretched her neck to take a peek into the playroom. Ryan was sitting on the floor quietly coloring. Of her three children, he was the most like his mama, choosing to draw or color over any other activity. He was still a bit young for the Museum of Fine Arts, but on the other hand, he might get a kick out of seeing some of the paintings and sculptures. Besides, it wasn't like she was planning on spending hours there walking through the massive building. She was interested only in this particular show. It wasn't everyday a Julien Henri exhibit came to town. She glanced back down at the article. This week only and the closest stop on his tour.

Ava looked at the piles of folded laundry to be put away and thought about everything on her to-do list for the day. It was the same as always, really: errands, cooking, cleaning, and kids.

"Oh screw it," she said to herself, getting up. "When do I ever do anything for myself?" She tore out the info for the exhibit and walked into the playroom. "Ryan, honey, come on. We're going back out."

Ryan seemed just as enthralled with the paintings at the exhibit as Ava. Well, perhaps enthralled was a bit of a stretch for a three year old. He seemed to have moderate interest. Okay—he wasn't complaining about being dragged around an art museum. Not yet at least. And there was certainly plenty to look at in the exhibit. Julien Henri was a master of his craft. After studying his work while Ava was a student at Wolfenson College, he'd become one of her favorite artists, second only to her true favorite, Claude Monet. Henri's love of impressionism and use of Monet's techniques were more than evident in his work. In fact, were it not for Henri's distinguishing signature, experts might argue that Monet himself painted some of the pieces now hanging on display. However, Henri was not simply a Monet copycat artist like so many others were. On the contrary, Henri was a talented painter who saw a modern world through impressionist eyes. He deserved every bit of the critical acclaim he'd received during his career.

Back in the day, Ava had tried desperately to get a Julien Henri piece in her gallery, but they were way beyond her reach. Most were just simply not for sale, and if they were, they sold through big auction houses, not small town galleries. She hadn't seen an original Henri painting in years and was completely mesmerized by this incredible collection.

Grabbing Ryan's hand, she walked over to the bench in the center of the room to sit. There was only one way to truly view an exhibit such as this one, and they were lucky it was a quiet Wednesday morning in the museum. Had it been a weekend, they would never have been able to just sit and soak up the view. After pointing out some of the nuances of each of the paintings—clearly all lost on her young son—Ava was content to relax in silence while looking around the room. She found herself getting lost in each piece, imagining Henri in his studio, brush in hand, as he created each work. What were his inspirations? How long did each painting take? Did he struggle with light and shadows as she often did when painting? Most importantly, why didn't she come here to the museum on a regular basis? Every second that passed left her feeling more and more relaxed.

A group of chatty teenagers, students on a school trip presumably, interrupted her thoughts as they filled the room, blocking her view.

She sighed loudly. So much for her stress-free morning.

"I guess that's our cue, buddy." When she looked over to where Ryan had been sitting, she discovered he was no longer there. "Ryan?" she called out, searching the room, trying to see through the crowd. Her heart raced as she jumped up and pushed people aside in a panic, continuing to call out his name. He was *just* here. *Wasn't he?* How long had she been zoned out?

"Ryan?"

"*Ryan!*"

12 TESSA

"What is it?" Nicholas asked, walking into the room as if nothing were wrong ... as if their entire world wasn't about to come crumbling down around them.

"Where's Sophie?" Tessa asked in a shaky voice, unable to take her eyes off her computer screen.

"In her room, still deciding what to wear. Apparently, the purple shirt didn't match the blue skirt, but she thought changing to the purple skirt would make her look like a grape, so she went with the red shirt, but then decided it would look better with pants, and for some reason that I'll never understand, she thought *I* would be able to give her advice on the matter. Does this usually happen every morning?"

Tessa stared blankly at the name on the message waiting to be opened.

"Sweetie, did you hear anything I just said? Are you okay? What's going on?"

"He contacted me," she whispered.

"Who?"

Tessa shut her eyes for a second, feeling all of the breath leave her lungs. She looked back at the screen and pointed with a quivering finger, unable to say his name out loud.

Nicholas placed his hands on his wife's shoulders. "Did you open it?" he asked in a soft voice.

She shook her head. "I can't."

"Tessa, look at me." He turned her around in her chair. "I love you, and I support you whatever you decide, but I really think you should read what he has to say. What if it's something important, like a health issue that could affect Sophie? You've always said that was a huge concern for you—not knowing the medical history of her father's side of the family."

"And what if he suddenly wants to come back into Sophie's life?"

"What if he does?" Nicholas asked. "She's been asking a lot of questions lately. She *wants* to know about her father. This may be her only chance to get to know him."

"She knows enough." Tessa turned back around. *Damn you, Scott. Why now?*

"She doesn't know much of anything, sweetie."

"Well, what was I supposed to tell her?" she asked, still keeping her voice low so her daughter wouldn't overhear from her bedroom upstairs. "That her father is a coward who ran off because he didn't want to be a husband to me or a father to her? That he disappeared and never once called to ask about her after she was born? Should I tell her how before we met you, we struggled and lived in a not-so-great neighborhood because her father never once paid us a dime of child support? Are these all the things I was supposed to tell her about her father? Because, believe it or not, despite my hostility—and I still have plenty—I somehow managed to keep all those redeeming qualities to myself. So yes, that's why she knows so little about her father."

"I'm sorry," Nicholas replied, resting his head on top of hers. "You're her mother. Whatever you decide to do, I'll of course stand by you. You know I just want what's best for Sophie … and you."

"I know," Tessa said. "You're the greatest thing that's ever happened to Sophie and me. Our lives are perfect right now. Our *family* is perfect right now. I just don't want anything to ruin it. Bringing another person into the mix could change everything."

"Are you two talking about having a baby?" Sophie squealed from the doorway, clasping her hands together. "I'm so excited!"

"What?" Tessa asked. While she was grateful her daughter hadn't heard the entire conversation, she now had to figure out how to do major damage control. Standing to block the computer screen, she looked at her husband. Just how *would* they explain the conversation to their daughter? She hated to lie. "No, Sophie. I'm sorry, no. Nicholas and I were just talking about—"

"Your mom and I were just talking about the possibility of introducing you to ... um," Tessa was trying to subtly shake her head as he continued, "a puppy."

"A what?" Tessa and Sophie asked together.

"That's right. I know you've been wanting a puppy, Sophie, and well, you're so good with both Aunt Ava and Aunt Holly's dogs. Maybe it's time we get you one of your own."

"Really?" she squealed again, her excited expression returning once more. "But you said person when I walked in. I heard you."

"Well," Nicholas said, keeping a calm voice, "that's because pets are like family members. Uncle Max refers to his dog as another one of his kids all of the time. You'll see once it gets here."

"And just when will that be, *sweetie*?" Tessa asked, wondering how this conversation went from no dog, to the *possibility* of a dog, to it already arriving.

"I'm not sure, to be honest," Nicholas answered. "Like I said, Sophie, Mom and I were just discussing it when you walked in. A puppy is a big responsibility. We'll talk some more about this later." He looked at his wife and winked, before blowing her a kiss, most likely in hopes of keeping himself out of the doghouse.

"Sophie, are you ready for school?" Nicholas asked. "It's time for us to get going."

"Yup," she replied, beaming. "This is turning out to be the best day ever. Bye, Mommy, can't wait to watch movies with you later."

"Me too, honey. Have a great day." Tessa gave her daughter a hug and kiss and watched as she went off to find her book bag.

"I'm sorry," Nicholas said once she left the room. "I couldn't think of anything else. Don't worry, I'll figure something out. A puppy around here might be fun."

Raising her eyebrows, Tessa shook her head in mock pity. "She's got you wrapped around her finger, that's for sure." She sighed and looked back to her computer screen. "You think I should read it, don't you?"

"I do, but ultimately the decision is yours. And remember, you don't owe him anything ... including a response. I love you."

"I love you, too," Tessa responded. "Now, can I trust you to take Sophie to school without promising her a pony or any other living creatures?"

"Scouts honor," he replied, holding up two fingers.

Tessa smiled as she listened to the sounds of her husband and daughter leaving the house. *Wait a second,* she thought, *he was never a Boy Scout.* She sighed and returned to the computer. Before she could give herself a chance to change her mind, she clicked to open the message.

Dear Tessa,

I hope this email finds you well. I know I'm the last person you ever expected to hear from. I saw your wedding announcement on our local news a while ago. I guess when you marry one of the richest men in the country word gets around. Your daughter was in the picture with you. Our daughter that is, although she looks just like you. I can't believe she's seven already. I probably have no right to ask this, but I'm going to be in town soon, and I was hoping I could come visit her.

All the best,
Scott

She slammed the cover to the laptop shut.

13 AVA

"Ryan!" Ava screamed again in a desperate attempt to find her toddler. The crowd in the museum continued to grow as more groups entered the main room of the Julien Henri exhibit. "Oh God, please be okay," she whispered as she ran into the next room toward a security guard standing in the corner.

She stopped suddenly, shocked to see her son standing in front of one of the paintings, with a complete stranger. Pointing to the canvas before them, her child was explaining the finer points of impressionism, which Ava had taught him earlier that morning, in his broken three-year-old speech.

"Ryan!" she yelled, pulling him toward her. "You can't run off like that. Mama was so worried about you."

"You said look at the paintings," he said, crinkling his nose. "And then you lost me."

Scooping him up in her arms, she hugged him tight. "I'm sorry, honey. I didn't mean— I'm here now. Next time don't go anywhere without me. Okay? Promise?"

The man he'd been talking to continued to stand, watching their conversation. "It's my fault," he interjected. "I should have realized and taken him over to the security guard right away. He just seemed to have belonged here."

Ava tilted her head, confused at what the man was saying to her. *Belonged here?*

"What I mean is, he didn't seem at all scared. In fact, he walked right up to me and began telling me all about the painting. About the colors, brush strokes, and shadows. He's really quite an art aficionado."

"He's not supposed to talk to strangers," Ava said with an irritated tone, holding Ryan even tighter. Who did this guy think he was? And yes, he should have brought him over to the security guard. Who sees a toddler *alone in a museum* and thinks that's okay? She shut her eyes for a second. Of course, who would let her toddler run off unattended in a museum? Maybe she was being a bit hard on this guy. "I'm sorry," she hastened to apologize, correcting herself. "Thank you for watching out for him. He does indeed seem to have taken a liking to the arts."

"I'm sure it's a reflection of your parenting," the man said, smiling. "You don't see many young ones at the Museum of Fine Arts these days, at least not without an electronic device in their hands. It's great when parents get their kids started at an early age."

"Oh, well ..." Ava felt heat rise to her cheeks. If he only knew she'd never brought either of her older two children here, and that this was her son's first visit. "I do love it here." It wasn't a complete lie.

"Gregory Douglas," the man said, holding out his hand.

Ava smiled. Of all the strange coincidences ... could it be? It had been quite a while ago, but she thought his voice sounded a bit familiar. "The artist?" she asked, shifting Ryan to her other arm in order to return his handshake.

"Yes. I'm in town for an exhibit of my own. Nothing this grand, of course, just a small showing at a local gallery. You're familiar with my work, then?"

"I am," she stated, smiling. How funny, after all these years. "I'm Ava. Ava Wallis. I used to run the Silver Leaf Gallery in California. You probably don't remember, but I helped arrange a big exhibit of yours about eight years ago. We never actually got a chance to meet face-to-face. I left town just before the exhibit ran, but I think we probably had about fifty phone conversations trying to set up all the details."

"Yes, of course I remember you, Ava. I was so disappointed when you told me you were leaving town. The exhibit was one of my best, thanks to your hard work. Well now, it certainly is a small world and a pleasure to finally meet."

"It is," Ava agreed, thinking how Gregory was nothing like she'd pictured all those years ago. She knew he was a bit older than her, but he gave off a much younger and hip persona with his stylish salt and pepper hair and tortoise shell glasses. He could easily be a model, especially with his flawless skin and sparkling green eyes. Not to mention his infectious smile, which she instantly returned. Suddenly, she realized her focus on his appearance left her completely distracted and at a loss for words. "Um ... so—"

"Mama, I'm hungry," Ryan interrupted, bringing Ava back into reality.

"Yes, sweetie," she said, shaking her head slightly, as if trying to remove any improper thoughts. "Well, Gregory, this was quite a surprise. It was a pleasure to finally meet, and again, thank you for watching out for my son."

"Actually, I was just about to go grab a bite to eat myself. Would you two care to join me?" he asked.

It was an innocent question, yet if felt so very dangerous to Ava. Despite the response she wanted to give, she shook her head and lied, "No, thank you. We're meeting friends."

"Well, maybe another time then." Reaching into his pocket, Gregory pulled out a postcard and handed it to her. "Shameless promotion, I know, but here's the information about my exhibit. The opening is in a few weeks. I came early to catch this show. I'm a big fan of Henri's. Anyway, it was a pleasure to finally meet, and I hope you can make it over to the gallery for the opening."

"Thank you," Ava said, her eyes darting from the card back to his face. "I'd love to be there." This time, she wasn't lying.

"Great, I look forward to seeing you." His eyes lingered on her long enough for her to feel her blush return, before he turned toward Ryan and patted him on the back. "I enjoyed our chat, little man. Maybe one day I'll have a chance to show you some of my paintings."

"Bye, mista," Ryan said.

"Good-bye," he chuckled.

Ava watched as Gregory left the exhibit before she put Ryan down beside her, still clutching his hand. In fact, she didn't think she'd be letting go of his hand anytime soon.

"You know him, Mama?" Ryan asked.

"I used to, a long time ago." She was still looking at the doorway Gregory had just walked through. "In another life," she added with a whisper.

14 HOLLY

"**A**re you sure you're doing okay?"

Holly forced herself to smile even though Ava couldn't see her on the other side of the telephone. It was an old trick her mother had taught her. No matter what your mood, if you were able to smile, your voice would come across as happy. She'd used it many times over the years, particularly during the time Ben was dating that floozy Michelle Floyd.

"Yes. Ben and I had a long talk this morning. I'm feeling much better now. Oh hey, remember that cabin I was telling you about?"

"The one you guys were going to go to this summer?" Ava asked.

"Mmm hmm. Ben's boss told him it's just been sitting up in the mountains empty, and he offered it to us anytime."

"So when are you going?"

"In a couple of weeks. We're going to make a long weekend out of it. We really need to get away, just the two of us."

"It sounds like heaven," Ava murmured wistfully.

"Well, maybe Max can take some time off, and you guys can spend a weekend up there, too. Like I said, it's empty, so I'm sure Ben's boss wouldn't mind. We'll watch the kids, of course. You two could use a romantic weekend away, right?" Holly waited, but there was no response. "Ava? Did I lose you?"

"What? No, I'm here."

"Is everything okay?" she asked, detecting the sound of a sniffle in her sister's voice. Was it possible she didn't want to go away for the weekend with Max?

"No, everything's fine. I think a weekend away sounds lovely. Perfect in fact. Just like things used to be."

Yes, there it was again. Another sniffle. "Ava, honey, something's wrong. I can hear it in your voice. Come on, talk to me."

"No, I'm fine ... and you have more than enough on your plate right now."

"Now you listen to me, Ava Haines Wallis," Holly said, her voice getting louder with each word, "A: I just got done telling you I feel much better, B: You're always there for me and Tessa, and you never let us help you, and C: You're always there for me and Tessa, and you never let us help you. Now tell me what's wrong. Right now."

"B and C were the same," Ava remarked.

"That's not the point," Holly told her. "Well, yes, that was the point. Come on. You don't always have to carry all of your burdens on your own. For once let someone else in.

"Okay," Ava said. Holly could hear her sigh before she continued. "I lost Ryan at the museum today."

"What?" Holly shrieked so loud the crystal in her china cabinet rattled. "Oh my God! Why are you so calm right now? Why didn't you call me?"

"Um … probably because you have a tendency to freak out a little. Everything is fine. We went to go see an exhibit, and he wandered into the next room without me realizing. I only took my eyes off him for a second. At least I think it was just a second. Oh, Hol, I completely lost track of time. To be honest, I don't know how long my son was lost. I mean, what if I hadn't found him? What if—"Ava's sobbing stopped her from finishing her sentence. "I'm a terrible mother," she finally said when she had calmed down a bit.

"No, you're not," Holly assured her, now feeling awful about her outburst. "You're one of the best mothers I've ever known. Scratch that. You are *the* best mother I've ever known. Every time I think about being a mom, you're the person I think of, the one I want to be exactly like. Don't beat yourself up. What happened today could have happened to anyone. The important thing is that Ryan is fine. See? This is why a weekend away is exactly what you need."

"There's more," Ava said with a hesitant tone to her voice.

"More?" Holly asked, not sure she was ready for part two of this story, but she had offered to be her sister's sounding board. Now was not the time for her to back down or overreact.

"Ryan was talking to a man when I found him. He was telling the man about the paintings … about things I had taught him."

"That's good, right? I mean, not good that he ran away, but good that he's so into art."

"The man was also an artist," Ava continued, ignoring Holly's last statement, "someone who was a client when I worked at the gallery on the West Coast."

"You knew him? That's random."

"I'll say. We'd never met face-to-face. We'd only spoken on the telephone." Ava explained to her sister the nature of their business dealings, and why they'd never had a chance to meet.

"What a strange coincidence. I have to tell you, Ava, this story is turning out much better than I expected. So, are you going to go to his opening?"

"I don't know," Ava said.

"What do you mean, you don't know? You just got done telling me how disappointed you were that you had worked so hard on setting up this guy's exhibit only to have to miss it. This sounds like a great opportunity for you to finally get to see his collection all together, even if it is arranged by someone else. You'll still get the same basic gist, won't you? Plus, it gets you out of the house without kids, which you really need, if you don't mind me saying. Are you worried about leaving Jenna alone with the kids?"

"No, Jenna will be fine. It's me I'm worried about," Ava responded.

"I don't understand."

"Hol, I couldn't take my eyes off the guy."

15 TESSA

"**N**ext!" Tessa yelled out as the actress left the stage.

"I'm afraid that's it, sweetheart. You've heard all thirty auditions. Please tell me one of them met your high standards and was good enough to be your leading lady."

"What?" Pulling off her glasses, she felt completely lost. Thirty auditions? She'd just sat through thirty auditions? She didn't recall a single one. Her mind was lost on the email from Scott. Shuffling through the pile of headshots and resumes, she paused at the face of a brunette with matching brown eyes looking back at her. *Dawn Thewer.* Funny, this entire time she'd pictured her lead as a blonde with blue eyes. Dawn's resume was light with only one real acting job in a small community theater. In actuality, on first glance, everything about this woman seemed wrong, but she didn't have the energy to sift through the credentials of each actress. She'd deal with her shortcomings once she got on stage. "Her," Tessa said, pointing to the resume in front of her. "Let her know rehearsals start first thing in the morning."

"So you were paying attention after all," Nicholas remarked, looking at Dawn's headshot. "I have to admit, when you didn't hire her on the spot, I was surprised … and nervous. She'll be thrilled, I'm sure."

Tessa managed to smile and threw her head back as she watched her husband leave the room. It was a lucky guess, but at least one thing was going right today.

She slid her laptop out of her briefcase and placed it on the table in front of her. Did she dare look again? Maybe she'd imagined the email. After all, she hadn't gotten a lot of sleep, and she'd had a lot of alcohol to drink last night—more than she'd had in a long time. Plus, despite all of the laughs, the SHOES meeting did get a bit intense at times. As much as she'd tried to avoid it, the topic of Scott's sudden departure did come up with her sisters, along with the pain that never fully went away. The possibility that her brain was playing tricks on her earlier, especially after the walk down memory lane they'd all taken last night, wasn't entirely farfetched.

She slowly opened the top to her computer and waited for the piercing beep, signifying her Wi-Fi connection. Reluctantly, she brought her eyes over to her email still open on the screen ... hoping ... praying, that despite the fact that Nicholas had seen it, the message never really existed.

Unfortunately, no amount of hoping and praying would make that wish come true. There it was, the email from Sophie's father that she'd read earlier—the first type of any contact from him since her pregnancy. Her heart raced as she read through it one more time.

"What do you think he wants?" Nicholas asked, his words startling her so much, she jumped clear out of her seat, nearly knocking the top of her head into his jaw.

"I don't know," she whispered as she sat back down, hand over her racing heart. "But I don't like it. I don't trust him, Nicholas."

"You could always just ignore him, pretend like you never saw his email. Frankly, he deserves it after the way he ignored you and Sophie all these years. Except ..."

Tessa turned around to look at her husband. She knew exactly what he was going to say, and he was right. *Damn it.* "Except then I'd be denying Sophie a chance to meet her biological father. And no, I wasn't going to say *real father,*" Tessa said, finishing his sentence. Standing up, she wrapped her arms around Nicholas' neck. "Lord knows you've been more of a real father to Sophie than that bastard ever will be. Thank you for that."

"I do love that little girl." He pulled Tessa in tight. "And I'm pretty fond of her mother, too."

"Fond?"

"Oh, okay, I'm head over heels, hopelessly in love. Better?"

"Much," she said, managing a smile before sighing. "I still don't know what to do. I mean, I know I have to tell Sophie I heard from him, but do I let her meet him? What if it's too much for her?"

"There's something you're forgetting here," Nicholas offered.

"What?"

"Well, there is a chance Sophie may not want to meet her father. If you were seven, would you want to meet the man who deserted you?"

"No, but I never worded it that way to her, not exactly at least. I believe the story I gave was that he wasn't able live near us, but that I was certain he loved her and thought of her often. I also told her that one day he might come back." Tessa cringed at the sound of the groan coming from her husband. "I wanted to tell her the truth, but she was so young, I didn't feel right telling her he was a coward who had no heart or conscience. I figured once she got older, then maybe I could explain it better. I don't know. Maybe, I'm the one who's the coward."

"No, you were trying to protect your daughter."

"It's just Sophie always looked so sad when I talked about him, and I wanted to give her something to hold on to. Like you said, I didn't want her thinking the asshole just up and left her." She paused to rub her temples. "Of course she's going to want to see him. She's been waiting seven years for him to return."

"I still think you should give her the option before you respond to his email. If you decide to respond that is."

"Yes." Tessa nodded. "It's the right thing to do. But she's not going to meet him alone. There's no way in hell that's happening."

"Agreed."

"So we'll wait for Sophie to get home from school and then talk to her?" Tessa asked, searching her husband's eyes for reassurance.

"Yes. Don't worry, sweetheart. Everything will be fine. I won't let anything happen to either of you. Promise."

"Okay." Tessa wished she could honestly believe her husband. "Tell me something, Nicholas," she asked, looking up at him.

"Anything," he responded, gazing back with adoring eyes.

"This woman we just hired to be the lead. She was good?"

"Outstanding," he said with a chuckle.

16 AVA

"So you thought the guy was hot, what's the big deal? You didn't throw him down in the middle of the museum and rip his clothes off, did you?" Holly asked, laughing.

"Of course not," Ava replied. It was just like her sister to make a joke out of something that seriously bothered her. There was a reason she kept most of her problems to herself, and this was a prime example. "It just made me uncomfortable that someone other than … Max?" Did she have her dates mixed up? She watched as his car drove up the driveway. She could have sworn he told her he wasn't coming home for another few days.

"Other than Max what?" Holly asked. "Ava? Are you still there?"

"I have to run. Max just got home. I'll talk to you later. I'm glad you're feeling better. Love you."

"Love you, too … and don't beat yourself up. You're allowed to think another guy is—"

Ava clicked end and tossed her phone on the counter before Holly could finish her sentence, although she knew exactly what she was going to say. For the record, she disagreed. In all her years of marriage, she had never once swooned over another man … well, not one that was standing two feet in front of her. Rock stars, nineteenth century artists, and actors on the big screen didn't count.

"Hey, Av," Max said, dropping his airline issued luggage in the middle of the living room. His coat, cap, and suit jacket quickly formed a pile on top of it, all to stay until his dutiful wife unpacked, sorted, laundered, and put everything away.

"Babe." She gave him a hug and quick peck on his lips before reaching for the cap and coat to hang up. "Are you home early?"

"Yeah. Two of my flights were cancelled at the last minute. Not enough tickets sold, so they consolidated them with other trips. I left you a message this morning. I guess you never got it?"

"Oh," Ava said, feeling flustered at his unexpected arrival. "No, I haven't had a chance to check my messages. But … this is great. I'm glad you're home," she said, smiling. Of course she was happy. Her husband was home. Where he belonged. She hugged him again and took his hands in her own. "The kids will be so excited. Ryan," she yelled. "Ryan! Come in the living room. I have a surprise for you!"

Little footsteps scrambled down the hall and stopped suddenly in the doorway to the living room.

"Daddy! You're home!"

"There's my little big guy," Max said, beaming at the sight of Ryan running toward him. Lifting him up, Max twirled him around before squeezing him tight and returning him down to standing. "I sure did miss everyone. So, Ryan," he started, squatting down to talk to his son, "what have you and Mommy been up to?"

"Oh, we had the funnest adventure this morning, Daddy!"

"Adventure, huh?"

Ava looked nervously from her son to her husband, wondering just what exactly Ryan was about to tell Max.

"Yup, Mommy took me to the museum this morning. We went to a big room where there were lots of paintings."

"Well," Max said, smiling, "that sounds like lots of fun."

"It was. Especially the part where Mommy fell asleep with her eyes open and was dreaming. That's when I met the man."

"What?"

Crap. There was no good way to explain the situation. "I wasn't sleeping or dreaming, sweetie," Ava began.

Max stood up, furrowed his brow, and looked at Ava. "So who was the man?" he asked.

"See what happened was," she started, "we went to see this exhibit that was a one week only show of Julien Henri. Well, you know how much I adore his work, right?" She waited for some sort of acknowledgement from her husband, but he only stood there with his arms crossed over his chest. Taking a deep breath, she continued. "Anyway, the place was pretty much empty, so we sat on the bench in the middle of the room. Just the two of us. I guess I kind of got lost in the pieces, because the next thing I knew, Ryan was in the next room having a discussion about the paintings. My little art lover."

"You didn't notice him wandering off?" Max asked with a raised voice and wide eyes.

"No, it's okay," Ava assured, rubbing his arm. "See? He's right here. Everything's fine."

"Ryan, why don't you go back to the playroom? Mommy and I need to catch up for a little bit."

"Okay, Daddy," he said before skipping back down the hall.

"I know what you're thinking," Ava said, hoping to calm her husband down before things got too out of control, "but he was honestly fine. I found him right away. He just wanted to look at some more paintings. We had a talk about not going anywhere without me."

"And hopefully about not talking to strangers. I'm guessing that's where the man comes in?" Max asked, running his hands through his hair.

"Well, that's the thing. He wasn't a stranger after all," she answered.

"I don't get it."

"Remember when we were getting ready to move here from California, and I was in the middle of setting up a big exhibit for that artist Gregory Douglas?"

"Sort of."

That meant no. She couldn't blame him, though. It was a crazy time in their lives. They were worried about the move back to Forest Hills, worried her pregnancy with Logan was taking too much of a toll on her, worried about finding enough time to properly care for Jenna, and worried the airline was about to make another round of massive cuts.

"Well, it was a huge exhibit, and a lot of work for me, but because of the timing of our move, I had to miss it in the end. Turns out the artist, Gregory Douglas, was visiting the museum today, and that's who Ryan wound up talking to. Quite a coincidence, if you ask me. Anyway, you should have seen him, Max," Ava said with a tiny laugh. "He was pointing to the paintings trying to explain the colors and brush strokes, like a real professional. It was so adorable."

"Are you referring to the part about how you lost our son or the part about how he was talking to someone he thought was a complete stranger? Because I'm really not finding anything adorable about this story, Ava."

"Max, I really think you're overreacting. I told you, he's fine, and Gregory—"

"What if it wasn't this guy Gregory, Av? What if it was someone who wasn't interested in learning about paintings? What if it was someone who snatched Ryan up and ran out the door with him? It only takes a split second."

As the reality of the situation hit her, tears streamed down her face. She could try to rationalize the events all she wanted, but the truth was she wasn't paying attention, and she'd gotten lucky. "I'm sorry," she whispered, shaking as Max wrapped his arms around her. "You're right, and I'm so sorry."

17 TESSA

The silence from the street was enough to drive Tessa insane as she sat on the couch and read yesterday's Arts and Entertainment section of the newspaper. The article in front of her was a review, but after five reads she couldn't say if was for a movie, book, recording, or play. She also had no idea if the review was positive or negative. The words only stared blankly at her, never registering into her subconscious.

On most days, the sound from the screeching brakes of the school bus would pull her out of whatever work she was engrossed in. She'd open the door for Sophie, give her a kiss, ask her how school was, and watch as she got started with homework with her high school babysitter for a minute or two before returning to the theater for several grueling hours of rehearsals. Today would be different. So very, very different. For starters, the bus was late … only three minutes, but to Tessa it felt like three hours. And there would be no afterschool babysitter. Not anymore. With Nicholas there to take over the business side of things, she could hold all of her rehearsals during school hours and be home for Sophie after school and at night. She peeked out the window for the twentieth time.

"Watching for the bus every two seconds is not going to make it get here any faster, you know," Nicholas told her, taking the newspaper out of her hand and exchanging it for a cup of hot tea. "It's herbal. The box said it was good for calming the soul. I figured you could use it right about now."

"You're so good to me," she replied, taking a sip. "It's perfect." As she placed the cup on the table, the sound she'd been waiting for jolted her out of her calm moment. "She's here." Tessa watched her daughter step off the bus.

Sophie bounded through the front door with the biggest smile on her face. "Mommy, I had *the best* day!" she said, full of energy and glee … her entire body radiating with excitement. "You're not going to believe it. First, Mrs. Cliffman chose *my* family tree art project for Community Month. She's going to hang it in the lobby for *thirty* whole days. *Everyone* will see it.

Then, I got picked to use the bongos in music. I've been waiting *all year* for my turn, and *then* I found out I came closest to guessing the correct number of jellybeans in the giant jar on Mr. McKinley's desk. So guess what I won?" She reached into her book bag and pulled out a giant sack of candy. "Yup, *all* the jelly beans. They're mine now!"

"Wow," Tessa said, taking the enormous bag from her. "You really did have a great day. That's wonderful, sweetie."

"Amazing," Nicholas chimed in with a huge grin. "So just how many jellybeans are there?"

"Eight hundred and thirty-seven. I guessed eight hundred and sixteen," she stated proudly. "Only off by twenty-one."

"Impressive," he said, raising his eyebrows. "This is definitely a day to remember."

"And it's not even done yet, because now Mommy and I get to spend the rest of the day together and have movie night! I've been waiting all day. What are we seeing first? Hey, can we eat jelly beans while we watch?"

Was this really happening? Did Scott really think he could just come and go as he pleased? She didn't have to tell Sophie. She could hit delete and pretend the email never existed. Her daughter would never know. They could snuggle on the couch, watch movies, eat jellybeans, and have the perfect ending to the perfect day. Except ... she'd know. It would forever hang over her head, and she'd never be able to forgive herself.

"Honey, before we get started, there's something I need to talk to you about."

"Is this about the puppy?" Sophie asked, hopping up onto the couch to snuggle in close to Tessa.

"No, we'll have to save the puppy talk for another time. There's actually something else we need to talk to you about."

"What is it?" she asked.

Tessa looked up at Nicholas. Nothing could hurt them now. Their lives were secure. She had this amazing man who adored both her and her daughter. Even without his riches, he made their lives complete. The money, house, and other perks were nice, but they weren't what mattered to Tessa. What mattered was that their lives were filled with an unconditional and unbreakable love. That alone was stronger than anything Scott could ever offer Sophie or try to take away from them. Still, just the thought of Scott's email was enough to suck her back into a dark place she'd tucked away years ago. Tessa concentrated on Nicholas' compassionate eyes and began to play with her daughter's hair as she spoke. "Sweetheart, Aunt Holly and Aunt Ava told me you were asking about Scott yesterday."

"Yes," Sophie said, a sadness pushing through the bubbly tone she'd had just seconds earlier. "I got upset at school when I was working on my family tree project and didn't have anything to write next to Scott's name. I mean, I know I have Nicholas, but I still don't understand why my other dad isn't around. Sally Hart's mom got remarried, and her first dad still visits her every weekend. She asked me why mine didn't, and then some of the other kids started teasing me about it."

"I'm so sorry that happened to you." When Tessa pulled her in for a hug, she could feel her eyes starting to well up. "I'm sure if Scott could have been here he would have been," she lied. She was always lying when it came to Scott, and it killed her to defend him. But in the end, she had only one goal: protecting Sophie from the pain of knowing her dad didn't care enough about her to stick around. She was determined to meet that goal, no matter what.

"I know, Mommy. It just makes me sad. You said one day he might come, and so far he hasn't."

"Sophie, if Scott does come to Forest Hills, do you think you'd want to see him?" Tessa asked.

"Of course," her daughter exclaimed, her voice perking up again. "I would love that. I've been waiting so long."

It was the answer Tessa both expected and dreaded. Nicholas continued to look at his wife with kind eyes and a caring smile. She nodded back at him and decided she would email Scott back to set up a meeting, establishing some strict and non-negotiable ground rules as part of the deal. Later. At the moment, she had more pressing matters to attend to: movie watching and jellybean eating with her precious daughter.

18 HOLLY

Soft music played in the background as the waiter filled their glasses. Holly sat back in her chair. It had been two weeks since she'd lost the baby. *Their baby.* She smiled, as she looked across the table at her husband. No matter how tough things were, she knew how blessed she was to have Ben in her life. He was her rock. He always would be.

"We really need to do this more often," she said, taking a sip of her water. Ben had asked if she wanted to order a bottle of wine, but she declined. She didn't need alcohol to ease her stress … not with Ben sitting right there across the table from her.

"I agree," he said, reaching over to take her free hand in his own. "Why don't we?"

"Well, for starters, we're sitting in The Urban Bistro," she told him, looking around the restaurant. Trendy pendant lights perfectly spaced gave just enough light to see the crystal and china place settings immaculately set at each table amongst bowls filled with colored water, lit tea candles, and floating flowers in contrasting colors to offset the linens. Bright gold ornate columns dispersed throughout the room brought a deep contrast to the walls, which were dark red and orange, with a splattered and uneven texture, giving it a rustic barn look. The restaurant was described as French fusion and the decor as shabby chic meets Versailles. At least that's what the full-page write-up in *Restaurant Weekly* said. "This place isn't exactly in our everyday dining price range."

"Or our price range at all," Ben said, staring at the menu with a strange look on his face.

"Babe, we're allowed to treat ourselves once in a while. Don't be such a spoilsport. The prices aren't that bad. Besides, I don't remember you complaining when you took *Michelle* here back before we were married, remember?" Just saying her name out loud made Holly's stomach turn. Michelle was one of the vilest women she'd ever met. She still couldn't believe Ben had fallen for her tricks. No, calling her a *woman* was too kind. Holly didn't want to insult her other women friends by lumping her into their category.

Michelle belonged in her own category: Disgusting, conniving, loathsome, *thing*. Much better.

"That's because she was paying," Ben reminded her. "She was my sugar mama."

"Actually, I have a different set of descriptive words put aside for her," Holly muttered, rolling her eyes. "But okay, if being a sugar mama is what it takes, then tonight will be my treat ... and let's not bring up that *thing's* name again."

"You're the one who mentioned ... Okay," he said, shaking his head, with the look of defeat Holly had seen so many times over the years. "Anyway, you do realize, of course, that all of our accounts are combined, so your money and my money is kind of the same. You know, that whole marriage thing?"

"Well fine, then. But don't say I didn't try to take you somewhere nice," she said with a smirk. "If it were up to you, we'd probably be eating at Roy's Rib Shack or something."

"What's wrong with Roy's Rib Shack?"

"No, it's great," Holly replied. "Nothing says romance like getting a big 'ole plastic bib slapped on you the minute you sit down."

"I know, right?" Ben asked. "Now if that's not service, I don't know what is. I don't see that happening here, do you? Seriously, do you think these people care if you spill some of their fancy sauce on your clothes? Nope. But they care at Roy's that's for doggone sure," he added, winking.

"Yeah, and don't forget the picnic table and benches covered in brown paper. It's all the rage in decorating. In fact, I was thinking of re-doing our entire house that way, so start saving the grocery bags."

"See that?" Ben replied with a huge smile. "I knew it was a classy joint. Only the best for my babe."

"Yeah," Holly agreed, "but the best part is that instead of soft music, we get serenaded by the belches from the people sitting at the next table. You're right, Ben, this place doesn't even come close. What was I thinking?"

"Listen," her husband moved his chair closer and nuzzled his face into her neck, "all kidding aside, if it's romance you're looking for, just wait until I get you alone next weekend at the cabin."

"Oh yeah?" Holly asked softly, leaning into his body. "Just what did you have in mind?"

"Well, Mrs. Oakes, I plan on completely sweeping you off your feet. I think you need a bit of pampering, and I'm just the guy who's going to make it happen. I don't want to give too much away, but there will be candles and your favorite Louis Armstrong CD. Did I mention my boss' cabin has a hot tub?"

Holly felt her breathing begin to slow as she closed her eyes and pictured the scene. "No," she replied in a low voice. "Are you sure we have to wait until next weekend?"

"I'm afraid we do," he said, whispering directly into her ear, "but there's no reason we can't go home and create our own romance. You know, it can be sort of a trial run for us. If you feel up to it. The doctor said it was your call."

"It's been two weeks. I'm ready," she replied, smiling. "Let's go."

"Now?" Ben asked, pulling away. "What about dinner?"

Running her hands through Ben's hair, Holly looked at her husband with a mischievous grin. Screw dinner. She needed her husband right now. "We can stop at Roy's Rib Shack on the way home and grab some take out for later," she said, laughing.

19 TESSA

"You're trembling," Nicholas whispered, holding on to Tessa's waist as they walked through the parking lot toward the diner.

"I'm okay," she answered softly. She wished it were true. In reality, her heart was beating so fast, it felt as if it would burst right through her chest and fly off into the clouds. Looking over to her daughter, she wondered if she felt the same way. Earlier, Sophie was downright giddy with excitement over the thought of meeting her biological father. She'd changed her clothes five times, wanting to make sure she looked absolutely perfect for him. Tessa prayed he didn't bail ... again.

When Tessa emailed Scott to say Sophie would meet him, she was surprised he didn't email her back right away. After all, he was the one requesting the meeting. But, as Nicholas calmly reminded her, not everyone checks their email daily, so she waited. On day two, she was starting to think maybe he had a change of heart and was beginning to feel relieved. On the third day, she was grateful she'd never mentioned the original email to her daughter. However, just as her guard was beginning to go down, on the fourth day, his response arrived: They were to meet at the diner on Brown Street a week from that Saturday at 11:00 a.m. It was the place he and Tessa used to eat on a regular basis. She hadn't been back since he'd left town. A calculated move on his part or the only place he could think of?

"Mommy, is that him?" Sophie asked, pulling on Tessa's arm as they walked through the front door.

A bell jingled as it closed behind them, rattling her nerves even further. Tessa scanned the room. "Where honey?" she asked. Almost eight years had gone by since she'd last seen Scott. Would she even recognize him?

"Over there." Sophie pointed to a balding man with a short beard wearing a flannel shirt, who sat alone in a booth, fiddling with his phone.

"I'm not sure," Tessa answered. The Scott she knew had a full head of hair and no beard. He looked up at her, and her heart suddenly skipped a beat. *Sophie's eyes.* All this time she thought Sophie had her eyes, but there was no doubt about it. She had Scott's eyes. "Yes, that's him," she said, barely able to get the words out. She clutched her daughter's hand as Scott rose and slowly approached.

"Tessa," he said, "I can't believe it's really you."

As he leaned in to kiss her on her cheek, Tessa took a step back and grabbed hold of Nicholas' arm with her free hand. How dare this man think he could touch her like they were old friends?

Her husband stepped forward. "I'm Nicholas," he said, "Tessa's husband."

"Right." Scott reached in to shake his hand. "I recognize you from the picture I saw. The guy with all of the businesses."

"And of course, this is Sophie," Nicholas continued, not responding to Scott's last remark.

"Hello, sir," Sophie said meekly.

"Sir? No need to be so formal, honey. I'm your daddy."

"No," Tessa said, feeling years of rage seep into her blood. "Nicholas is her daddy. You don't know the first thing about—" She stopped at the touch of her husband's hand on her shoulder and took a deep breath. This was neither the time nor the place. "I'm sorry," she said, before bending down to look at Sophie. "Sweetheart, you can call him whatever you're comfortable with."

"Is Scott okay?" she asked.

"It's fine," he responded.

"Y'all together?" a waitress asked, holding a stack of menus across her chest.

Tessa looked over to the booth where Scott had been sitting. He'd originally asked to meet Sophie alone, but Tessa refused. In the end, she agreed her daughter could sit with him solo, as long as she and Nicholas were nearby. A couple in the booth directly behind Scott's was just getting up to leave. "Can my husband and I take that booth over there?" she asked, pointing to the now vacated space. Grabbing Sophie's hand, she headed over without waiting for an answer.

"We're right behind you," she told Sophie, watching as her daughter slid in the booth behind them. "And we can hear everything," she added, glaring at Scott.

"Why are these walls so damn high?" Tessa asked. As soon as she and Nicholas sat down, she realized she couldn't see her daughter or Scott over the separation between the two booths. She'd purposely taken the seat facing them so she could watch, but now the only thing she could see was her husband and a wall of quilted red pleather.

"I'm assuming for privacy," Nicholas said.

"Maybe we should switch seats. I can't hear a thing from over here."

"Sweetheart, relax. Sophie has her back to me. I can hear, and she's doing fine. They can't go anywhere without walking by us. How about some coffee?"

"But what's she saying?" Tessa whispered. She was already on edge ... coffee was the last thing she needed.

Leaning back into the seat, Nicholas put his fingers up to his lips to shush her. Tessa sighed as she waited for her husband to report something back to her.

A gum-chewing waitress, who didn't seem to understand they were on a covert spy mission, broke the silence. "What can I get you?" she asked, snapping her gum as she talked.

"Two coffees please," Nicholas responded.

"Decaf," Tessa instructed.

"And I'll have two eggs over easy. Do you want anything to eat, sweetheart?"

"No, thank you."

The waitress wrote everything down, snapped her gum a final time, and stepped over to Sophie and Scott's booth to take their order.

"So?" Tessa asked, getting impatient.

"It's just been small talk so far. Scott's been asking about school, activities, friends—things like that." He leaned his head back and listened again. "He just ordered her a chocolate milkshake with extra whipped cream."

"He's trying to win her over with sweets?" she asked.

"Can't really blame him there," Nicholas replied. "It's not like he has any redeeming qualities. Anyway, don't look so worried. Think of this as a good thing. Scott's going to leave town again, Sophie will stop asking so many questions, and everything will go back to normal. You'll see."

"I hope you're right," Tessa said as the waitress walked away. "I really hope you're right."

20 AVA

"**H**as Sophie said anything?" Ava asked.

The three sisters stood around Holly's bed and stared at the pile of clothes. They were supposed to be helping her pack for her romantic weekend away with Ben, but so far all they'd managed to do was empty the entire contents of her closet and dresser onto her bed.

"Not really," Tessa responded, holding up an olive green shirt. She crinkled her nose and returned it to the closet. "She does want to see Scott again, though."

"Are you okay with that?" Holly asked.

"Do I have a choice? At this point, if I say no, I look like the jerk. Besides, I know Sophie still has a lot of questions she was too shy and nervous to ask at their first meeting."

"Like why he was an asshole and coward?" Holly rolled her eyes and pulled a pink sweater from the bottom of the pile. Nodding, she folded it and placed it neatly in her suitcase.

"I'm pretty sure she wouldn't word it that way, but something like that, yes," Tessa said. "He's the one who opened this can of worms. If she wants to go there, I'm not going to stop her. I'm sure she can't help but wonder why he stayed away for seven years. I know that's what I'd want to know."

"Do you?" Ava asked. Life was so much easier when she had her sisters' problems to focus on.

"Do I what?" Tessa asked.

"Do you want to know why he stayed away for seven years?"

"Me personally? I've asked myself that question a million times since he left, but honestly, after seeing him at the diner, I no longer care. Of course, Sophie certainly deserves an explanation. If you ask me, the better question is *why did he decide to come back?* I don't like it one bit."

"What are you going to do about it?" Ava asked. She knew her youngest sister so well. Tessa didn't sit back and let circumstances just happen. She needed to stay one step ahead. Especially where her daughter was concerned.

"I don't know," she replied, "but he's not going to hurt Sophie again. Not on my watch. He needs to know this mama bear is not about to let her cub out into the wild with the big bad wolf."

"I think you're confusing your nursery rhymes," Ava told her.

"Oh, you know what I mean," Tessa said, waving her arms. "Anyway, enough about me, what's going on with you? Holly mentioned you ran into an old flame or something? Does Max know?"

Tessa's comment took Ava by surprise. Gregory Douglas was hardly an old flame. In fact, up until two weeks ago, she'd never thought of him in any way other than a client. Actually, up until recently, she hadn't thought about him in years. Not that she was thinking of him differently now. He was just someone she happened to run into, who happened to be attractive. There wasn't anything more to it. She was grateful he'd been there for Ryan at the museum and even more grateful Max had dropped the whole *losing Ryan* issue after her explanation.

"Earth to Ava," Tessa called, giving her a little nudge back to their conversation. "Care to let the rest of us into your little daydream?

"No ... I mean, there's nothing to tell." Glaring at Holly, she continued, "And I didn't run into an old flame. I ran into an old *client.*"

"A hot client," Holly added with a flirty wink.

"He was somewhat good-looking," Ava corrected, "but so what. I'm married. *Happily married.* Tessa, don't you work with good-looking actors all day long?"

Her youngest sister shrugged and nodded.

"Well, it's the same thing. No big deal," she said, in a voice she hoped sounded somewhat convincing. She wasn't in the mood to have a conversation about feelings she may or may not be having about a virtual stranger. Her sisters always blew everything out of proportion. She never should have said anything to Holly. "Anyway, looks aside, he's an amazing artist, and he's opening his exhibit here in Forest Hills soon. I'm hoping Max and I will be able to go. I didn't realize how much I missed the art world until I took Ryan to the museum a few weeks ago." Sighing, she looked down, pretending to sort through clothes before her sisters noticed her sad expression. She never was very good at hiding her feelings.

"It was always your passion," Holly reminded her.

"My family is my passion now, and with Max's schedule ... well, there's no way I could go back to that world. It would be too difficult to juggle. No, I really do love my life. It's just ... being in the museum made me realize ... well, maybe I can make time for both." Smiling, this sudden revelation that she *could* make time for art made her feel much better about the situation. "Starting with my friend's exhibit."

"Oh, so he went from client to friend now?" Tessa teased.

Shaking her head, Ava picked up a pile of clothes and threw them at her youngest sister, who promptly threw a second pile back.

"Hey!" Holly yelled. "I just folded those." Seeing that neither sister was paying attention as they continued to giggle and throw clothes, she added, "Oh what the hell," and grabbed a bunch of clothes so she could join in the fun.

21 TESSA

Tessa's phone buzzed just as her new leading lady, Dawn Thewer, finished rehearsing her lines to the final scene of the first act. Her performance was once again flawless. She wished all of her actors were this easy to direct. In fact, she could hardly call it directing. Dawn had pretty much nailed it on her first run.

"Take five," Tessa yelled across the stage, as she walked to her tiny office. She clicked on the message to read the incoming email. It was from Scott and no doubt contained details about the where and when he wanted to meet Sophie next.

Tessa,

Please call me. I'm afraid I've run into a bit of a snag.

Scott

Sighing, she put her phone down on her desk. On the one hand, a snag could mean he wasn't coming again—which was fine by her—but on the other, she had Sophie to think about. Her daughter was bouncing off the walls excited for another visit. It was all she'd been talking about. *Just great.* A snag would not bode well. Picking her phone back up, she dialed the number he listed.

"It's me, Tessa," she said, upon hearing his greeting.

"Thanks for calling me."

She waited for him to explain his cryptic message, but instead, only an uncomfortable silence hung over the line.

"So you wanted me to call you?" she finally asked. Apparently she was going to have to take the lead in this conversation.

"It was great to see you last weekend," he responded. "I forgot how beautiful you were."

Was he serious? So his email was just some kind of ploy to get her to call so he could flirt with her?

"Scott, I'm really not in the mood—"

"No, what I meant was Sophie is beautiful, and it's clear she gets her looks from you. Sorry, I'm just nervous. I haven't been able to stop thinking about her since the weekend. We didn't get a chance to talk, you and me that is, but I wanted to thank you for letting me meet her … and also for everything you've done for her."

"You mean you wanted to thank me for being a loving and responsible parent to my daughter?" Tessa asked.

Once again, silence from the other end of the phone filled the air.

"Yes," a barely audible voice replied.

A snicker escaped her lips. Not that she tried to keep it at bay. Why should she? It was bad enough Scott ran out on her when she was pregnant with Sophie just weeks before they were to walk down the aisle, but to never even call or check up on them after Sophie was born? To just disappear as if they never existed? Wasn't he even the tiniest bit curious about his own child? His own *flesh and blood?*

"I don't know what to say," he added, with the same muffled tone.

"Well, you better think of something," Tessa said, "because Sophie's got plenty of questions, and now that the two of you have gotten the small talk out of the way, you can expect she'll be looking for some answers when she sees you next. When will that be, by the way?"

"Well, about that," Scott said.

Finally ... they were getting to the reason behind the email. "Ah yes, the snag you mentioned. So ... what's the deal?"

"Well, the thing is," he started, sounding a bit more like his old self, "I was hoping to come in a few weeks, but I'm not sure that's going to work now."

Tessa closed her eyes and shook her head. No. He was not going to desert and disappoint her daughter again. He was coming to visit her even if it meant finding him and dragging him to Forest Hills herself.

"Let me explain something to you, Scott," she began, willing herself to keep her cool, "there is a seven-year-old little girl waiting to see you. You've already abandoned her once. You're not going to do it a second time."

"I know that, but—"

"I'm not finished," Tessa continued. "Almost eight years ago now, you walked out on me knowing this little person that *you* fathered was about to enter the world. You didn't call, you didn't visit ... hell, I'm not even sure if you knew if you had a son or daughter to be honest. And yet, for reasons that I still haven't figured out, last week you felt compelled to come meet her. So now, I've got a daughter who thinks she's got a father who now *wants* to be a father. Someone who can keep his promises this time. This is a child we're talking about ... your child. It's all or nothing, Scott. So what's it going to be? Because if you walk out of her life again, don't expect to be welcomed back by either one of us."

"I know that," he said. "All of it. And I want nothing more than to be a father to Sophie. That's why I emailed you initially. What I'm trying to explain is that since last weekend, I lost my job. The company I work for got mixed up in some bad investments and had to make some deep cuts across the board. I was one of the casualties. It was completely unexpected. Anyway, until I figure out my job situation, I can't spend the money to come out there again, at least not right away. "

"When?" Tessa asked. If it was anyone else she'd feel bad for them, but not Scott. She honestly felt no remorse. He was a college graduate. Surely he could find a decent job. Plus, didn't he have any savings from the job he'd had? He couldn't have had much in expenses. He certainly didn't have payments of child support to Sophie as an expense. Just what had he been doing career-wise with his life all these years?

"I don't know when," he replied. "Like I said, I need to get settled with a new job first. It could take a while. Tell Sophie I'm really sorry."

"No!" Tessa said sharply, without a second thought. Her daughter would not be disappointed again. She'd get at least one more meeting. Sophie deserved a chance to have her questions answered. "I'll arrange for a wire with enough to cover your travel expenses. I expect you here Saturday at 11:00. Same location. Don't be late."

22 HOLLY

"Three bags?" Ben asked, looking at the arsenal of luggage lined up at the front door. "You do realize we're only going away for two nights."

"Which is three days," Holly added. "It's a bag a day. So what? You know how unpredictable the weather can be in the mountains."

"For the record, we're going to be alone all three days. If it were up to me, you'd be naked the entire time and wouldn't need any clothing at all."

"Well lucky for me, it's not up to you. But don't you fret, my love, your needs will be well taken care of." Holly nipped Ben's ear and rubbed her hand just along his inner thigh. It was a subtle move, yet guaranteed to drive him wild.

His sharp intake of air let her know just how effective it truly was. "Let me guess," he said, letting out the breath to presumably calm himself. With a second deep breath and a slight grunt, he lifted the first suitcase with two hands. "Your sisters helped you pack. Is there anything left in your closet?"

"Just that olive green shirt you don't really like," she said, smiling wide. "I'll bet you're wishing we got that luggage set I originally wanted. Remember? The one with the wheels?"

"Nope, I'm fine." He began struggling to get the bag out the door.

"Do you want a hand?"

"No, no," he replied with a grimace and gritted teeth. "I've got this."

"You sure do, and may I say thank you for giving me a fabulous view of your rippling muscles under that shirt you're wearing." Holly followed Ben outside and playfully patted his behind before giving his arm a squeeze. "You will be duly rewarded later for your hard work."

"I'm not sure I'll be able to move later." Lifting the bag with one final heave to get it into the trunk of his car, he groaned. "What's in here, bricks?"

"Only a few," she teased, walking into the house to get the second bag. Dragging it behind her, she brought it up close to the car as Ben continued to fiddle with the first suitcase. Might as well help the poor guy. After all, a resulting back injury would certainly put a damper on their romantic getaway. "I can get the last one." She smiled a playful grin. "Why don't you lift this into the trunk using only your pinky and give the neighbors a show of your true manhood."

"I've got a better idea," he said.

Before she could blink or even realize what had happened, he picked Holly up and laid her back on the hood of the car, passionately kissing her with her hands pinned over her head. Her shallow breaths slowly returned to normal as he pulled away slightly.

"Touché," she whispered. "How long until we get to the cabin?"

"Three hours. Two and a half if I speed."

"Okay," she replied, her voice still breathy. "Speed it is. I'll get the last bag, you start the engine."

"I think I already have," Ben laughed.

"I was referring to the car," she said, shaking her head as she walked into the house once more. Thankfully, the third bag was the lightest of the bunch, which meant it was the most important of the three. It held her extensive collection of sexy lingerie. She locked up the house, put the bag in the trunk, and slid into the passenger seat, where Ben was ready and waiting to hit the road. "Hey," she asked, as he pulled out of the driveway, "where's your luggage? Aren't you taking anything?"

Motioning to the backseat, he pointed behind him to a small duffel bag. "This, my love, is how you pack for two nights."

"Yeah, yeah." Rolling her eyes, Holly settled in for the long drive.

Music and conversation helped pass the time as they drove out of town making their way toward the expressway. A glimpse of her reflection in her window made her smile. She looked content, but not in a bored, stuck in a rut sort of way. It was the look one had when they'd reached a place of pure happiness and relaxation. Looking over to her husband as he drove up the highway ramp, she realized he had the same expression she did. Life was good.

"Ben?"

"Yeah, babe?" he asked, as he looked behind him to check oncoming traffic in order to merge on to the busy road.

"I know we said we weren't going to talk about babies and stuff," she replied, "but I've been thinking about what you said, about Nicholas helping us financially if we wanted to try another round of IVF."

Ben quickly glanced at Holly with a surprised look on his face before bringing his attention back to the road. "It's okay, babe. I understand where you're coming from, I really do. Going through ... well, we've just been through something traumatic, and we still need time to heal. That's why I think this weekend away is going to be so great for us. You don't think I'm upset about it, do you?"

"No, at least, I don't think so, but that's not why I brought it up," she explained.

"Okay … I'm not sure I understand."

"What I'm trying to say is that I changed my mind. After we get back home from this trip, let's give him a call. I want to give it another try."

"Holly," Ben darted his eyes quickly at her, "are you sure? I don't want you to do this for me. You have to make certain this is what *you* want. Is this what you want?"

"Yes. That's what I'm trying to tell you," she said, laughing. "This is what I want. For me *and* for you. *For us.*"

"Oh, babe." Ben reached over to take her hand with his right while keeping his left firmly on the wheel. He looked over at her for just a second and said, "You have no idea how happy this makes me. Thank you."

The last thing Holly remembered were the taillights of the tractor-trailer that had stopped short in front of them and the grinding sound of metal on metal as their car smashed up against it.

23   AVA

Ava watched her two boys play together in the backyard. While she couldn't hear them, she could tell just by the expression on their faces they were enjoying the nice weather and each other's company.

Back when she learned her second child was a boy, she was admittedly disappointed. It wasn't that she didn't want a son, she just didn't really know that much about taking care of little boys. With the exception of her father, a few dates, and her husband, she'd spent her entire life around girls. But she quickly learned that little boys were cuddly creatures who loved to get messy and give lots of kisses. Her heart, already stretched to the max upon the birth of Jenna, grew even bigger the day Logan was born, and once more with Ryan.

"I keep telling Ryan he has to keep his hands cupped if he wants to catch the ball."

Ava startled at the sound of the voice behind her, nearly dropping the dish she'd been washing into the sink.

"Max! You're home early. I didn't hear you come in. I wasn't expecting you until dinner time."

Wrapping his arms around her waist, he kissed her lips and explained, "My last flight got detoured ... there are some nasty storms down south. Anyway, we landed early, and here I am. I hope I gave you enough time to kick your boyfriend out."

"Oh, stop," she replied, kissing him back. "The only boys here are the ones you helped make. My boyfriend left hours ago." Winking, she gave him another kiss.

"Gross!"

Ava looked over to her daughter standing in the doorway ... a look of pure disgust on her face.

"*Oh, hi Dad! Welcome home. It's great to see you,*" Max said in his best teenage girl voice, still holding Ava close.

"Seriously," Jenna quipped, glaring at them, "do you have to do that in front of everyone?"

Max raised one eyebrow. "We *were* alone until *you* barged in. And last I checked, this is my house. I can pretty much do whatever I want, wherever I want."

Looking back to Ava, he kissed her again—this time a wet, sloppy, noisy kiss.

"Whatever," Jenna said with that tone all kids seem to have the minute they turn double-digits. "Mom, when you're done making out with Dad, can you tell me what time you need me to babysit tonight?"

"Babysit?" Max asked, pulling away slightly. "Did I forget about plans for this evening?"

"Sometime after dinner," Ava told her daughter. "Thanks."

"Okay," she said. "Oh and hi, Dad, welcome home. It's great to see you." Grabbing an apple out of the fruit bowl, she turned and walked out of the kitchen.

"Well?" Max asked again "What are these plans?"

"I mentioned it to you before you left. It's for the exhibit of the artist who I ran into at the museum with Ryan a few of weeks ago."

"You mean the day you lost Ryan, and *he* got lucky and ran into the artist you knew, when God knows what really could have happened to him."

Ava closed her eyes for a second. This conversation was not getting off to a good start, but now was not the time for an argument about the events of that day.

"Anyway," she continued, hoping they could quickly move past that part of the story, "this artist, Gregory Douglas, was in town because he was preparing for his own exhibit. The opening is tonight, and he invited us to go, as his personal guests. Remember?"

Max shook his head and sat down at the kitchen table. "Right. I guess I forgot. I'm sorry, babe, but I'm really beat. I just came off a six-hour flight, and I haven't been home in days. I just want to watch the game tonight and get some shut-eye."

She nodded. It was what he did every time he came off of a long shift. Every. Time. Except this one time, *she* wanted to do something different—with him—as a couple.

"What about what I want?" she asked. The words came out without her giving them any thought, but they needed to be said. "Max, being back in that museum did something to me. I can't explain it, but I miss that scene. The pieces, the smell of the paints, talking with artists, the mechanics of the exhibit itself, everything." Sitting down at the table, she took her husband's hand in her own.

"Don't these things last a few days? Why do we have to go tonight?"

It was like talking to a complete stranger. Max knew opening night was a big deal; the night everyone got dressed up to celebrate the artist and his or her work. It was a party, mixed with art, and she wanted to be a part of it. Besides, tomorrow he'd have another excuse, and then another. *There was always something.* "Tonight's the opening. Look, I know I chose to give up that life to raise our family, and I don't have any regrets. However, now that the kids are older, I need to start carving out more time for myself. I need to live and breathe art again."

"You're saying you want to go back to work?" he asked.

"No. I don't know, I haven't thought about that. What I'm talking about is going out, to events like the one we were invited to tonight. It's something we haven't done in years. Don't you remember how much we enjoyed doing that together? We never seem to go out anymore. I miss that, Max. I miss you."

"I'm sorry, but I really am wiped. Tonight the only date I want is one with my lazy boy chair and big screen TV. Why don't you call Tessa? I'm sure she'll go with you."

"Never mind." Ava sulked out of the kitchen, frustration, anger, and disappointment all crowding her brain, trying to make sense of her husband's words. Sitting on the couch she tried to remember when exactly it was he'd changed so much. Her thoughts would have to wait as she answered the phone.

"Ava?" the frantic voice said. "It's Tessa. I'm on my way to the hospital. There's been an accident."

24 HOLLY

"**M**rs. Oakes, the doctor would really like to examine you." The nurse put her hand on Holly's shoulder only to have it shrugged away, *again*.

"I told you I'm fine," she said, eyes glued to the door in the waiting room.

Several hours ago, they'd arrived at the hospital by ambulance where they rushed her husband into surgery. She'd tried to run down the hall after him, but an orderly held her back as she screamed and sobbed to let her go. Eventually, she was able to calm herself down enough to talk to a string of doctors ranging from medical students to internists to give them Ben's history and tell them what little she could remember from the accident. Somehow she managed to convince them, that despite the bloody bandage the EMS had placed on her forehead, she felt absolutely fine. Ben was the only thing she cared about. When they'd found him at the scene he was bloodied, unconscious, and barely breathing.

Now, she was just waiting. The nurse had brought her into a room reserved for families. It was there she realized she was alone. She gave the nurse Tessa's name and number as next of kin for some reason. Maybe it was because of her two sisters, her younger one always had such a special bond with Ben. Tessa told the nurse not to worry, she would take care of making the necessary calls to Ava and both her and Ben's parents. She arrived at the hospital in record time.

"Holly," Tessa said, grabbing hold of her sister's hand, "how are you holding up?"

She heard the words, but didn't respond.

"Sweetie, let me get you some coffee. I'm sure the doctor will have him back as soon as possible."

Oh, how she wished that was true. "As they rushed him in," Holly said, slowly turning her red and swollen eyes toward her sister, "the doctor ..." She stopped, not sure she could say the words out loud.

"The doctor what?" Tessa asked.

"He told me I should be prepared to say good-bye to my husband," she continued. "Before you got here, the hospital clergy came by to help me pray."

"Oh my God," Tessa said, her voice wavering with fear. She wrapped her arms around her sister. "But he's in surgery. He has been for a while. That means there's hope. They wouldn't be working on him this long if they didn't think there was a chance."

Nodding, Holly's expression remained stoic. "Yes, there's a slight chance."

"Okay then," Tessa said, sounding more like her self-assured self. She softly stroked Holly's trembling arm. "Okay. We just have to be strong and hold on to that ... together ... for Ben. Because he's a fighter. We both know that. I mean, look at all the things he's fought for over the years for both of us, and now he's going to fight for himself. I know he can do this, and you know this, too. Right?"

Before Holly could respond, two weary looking doctors, still in surgical scrubs entered the room. "Mrs. Oakes?" one of them asked.

"Yes?" Holly said, willing herself to stand up.

"Your husband is resting in the ICU. He had substantial internal bleeding which we were able to control. He also has several significant fractures in his right leg. We were able to do some temporary repairs. However, he'll need an orthopedic consult as soon as possible. He's still unconscious, but you can see him now. Just briefly though, he's quite weak."

Ben lay in the hospital bed, eyes closed, tubes and wires coming out of him. Around him machines rhythmically beeped, displaying numbers and graphs ...

the only confirmation Holly had that he was actually breathing. His face was barely recognizable under the blood and bruises covering his swollen skin.

Leaning over, she kissed his forehead, taking a moment just to silently thank God. Then, in the strongest voice she could gather she said, "Ben? It's me, Holly. I love you, sweetheart. You're banged up pretty good, but I know you're going to pull through this. You *have* to pull through this." She ran her fingers through his hair and continued, "They told me earlier I needed to say good-bye to you." Wiping her tears with her hand, she took a deep breath and tried to calm herself. Now was not the time to break down. She needed to be strong for the man she loved. "But I told them no. It's not your time, babe. We've got big plans together, you and me. Remember what we were talking about in the car? We still have so many memories to make together and so many more milestones to celebrate. I know you can hear me, Ben. I know you're strong enough to fight this. I'm going to fight with you. I promise. We're a team. Don't ever forget that. Don't ever forget how strong our love is." She backed away and nodded to the nurse who was waiting patiently to check his vitals. "I love you, babe," she said quietly while she backed out of the room. "You got this."

Tears flowed down her face as she turned around and buried herself in Tessa's shoulder.

"Come on," Tessa said, putting her arms around her sister. "Let's go find that coffee."

"Holly!" Ava shrieked as she ran down the hallway toward her with Max on her heels. "Are you okay? What happened? Where's Ben?"

Holly was grateful for her younger sister, who put her hand up to stop their oldest sister in her tracks. "She's fine," Tessa answered. "Just a bit shaken up. I'm sorry I couldn't tell you more on the telephone when I called you. I didn't know myself. The nurse wouldn't give me any details. All I knew was that they were in a nasty accident with a tractor-trailer."

"Oh honey," Ava said, giving Holly a hug. "I'm so relieved you're okay. I was so worried." Looking around, Ava asked the question Holly knew was coming, yet dreaded answering. "What about Ben? Is he all right?"

Her entire body tensed as she tried to think of the words to use. *He's okay, Hol. He's going to be just fine.* As long as she believed it, it would be true. As long as she said the words out loud, it *had to be* true. "He'll be okay, also," she said, looking at Tessa for reassurance. Taking a deep breath, she added, "He just got out of surgery. He was in bad shape, broken bones and internal bleeding. He's in recovery now in the ICU and still unconscious. But he's going to be okay." She nodded with confidence as she said each word in the last part of her statement slowly and with purpose.

"Oh thank God," Ava replied, hugging her sister close. "We were so worried."

"We're just on our way to find some coffee," Tessa explained. "Holly, you could probably use some food, too. When was the last time you ate something?"

"I don't know," she answered. "This morning maybe? I'm not hungry. My stomach's a mess. I really just want to sit here and wait for Ben to wake up. And what if the doctor needs to talk to me?"

"Okay," Tessa murmured and patted her arm. "You stay, and I'll bring some food back for you. You have to keep your strength up, and you also should let the doctor look at you. At the very least, have them check out the cut on your forehead."

Lifting her hand up, Holly felt the dampness through the bandage the EMS workers had put on her at the site. Blood, no doubt, was starting to seep through. "I'm fine, honest. It's just a scrape. It doesn't even hurt." That part was true—she didn't feel a thing since her entire body was numb after what she'd just been through.

25 TESSA

Sophie sat at the kitchen table. She appeared to be deep in thought as she wrote, erased, and wrote some more. From the couch in the living room, Tessa watched her daughter as she tried to re-group for their meeting with Scott. The last several hours had been an emotional roller coaster for Tessa and her family. She hoped Holly was finally getting some much-needed sleep. Truth be told, she could use a good eight hours herself. At this point, she'd even take three or four.

Shortly after Ava came to the hospital, a parade of people streamed in. Nicholas arrived first. He wasn't going to, but had felt hopeless waiting at home, so he knocked on their neighbor's door in a panic. She was a sweet older woman who was quite fond of Sophie. She agreed to look after her so he could join his wife at the hospital. After that, parents arrived, starting with a very frantic Mr. and Mrs. Oakes, followed quickly by her own parents ... both just an hour's drive away. She knew it would be too much on Holly to have to retell the story several times over, so Tessa took care of that job, while Ava and Nicholas tried to keep Holly distracted. After a couple of hours with no news, Nicholas returned home to Sophie, giving strict instructions to call if Ben's condition changed, while Tessa's parents drove Max home so he could relieve Jenna of babysitting duty. Her parents then went back to Holly's house where they would stay the night with Ben's parents, who first stayed at the hospital another few hours ... waiting.

Somewhere around midnight Ben finally opened his eyes. His only words were, "Holly." His eyes fluttered back closed the moment her name escaped his lips. At three a.m. he opened his eyes once more, this time appearing to be slightly more alert. At eight a.m. Ben's doctor convinced Holly he was stable enough for her to go home to get some sleep. Ava took her back to her house, seeing as though her and Ben's home was occupied with her parents and in-laws. Tessa left with them to return home to Nicholas and Sophie.

"I just got off the phone with William— Dr. Golden," Nicholas said, taking a seat next to Tessa on the couch.

"Is that the specialist you know?" she asked.

"Yes," Nicholas replied. "He arrived at the hospital this morning and has already spoken with Ben's doctor about taking over his treatment going forward. He's top in the country for spinal injuries, and his partner, an orthopedist with an impeccable reputation, is flying in later this afternoon.

"Spinal injury?" Tessa asked. "I thought he broke his leg and had internal bleeding."

"He had severe swelling in his spinal cord as well," Nicholas said. "Holly told me last night when I offered to help. I think she was so overwhelmed with everything, she just couldn't emotionally deal with it all."

"Thank you for doing this for her ... for all of us."

"We're family. That's what we do," he said, taking her in his arms. "And Ben is more than a brother-in-law to me, you know. He's the one who got us back together when I thought I'd lost you. Holly, too, of course, but mostly Ben. He loves you so much, Tess."

"I know," she responded, wiping her husband's tears. "I feel the same way. It's like you said. He's more than a brother-in-law. He's really one in a million. If he doesn't make it, I'll kill him," she snickered and reached for a tissue to wipe her own tears and sighed. "I'm trying so hard to stay strong for Holly, but I'm really scared, Nicholas."

"I know, so am I," he said, letting out his own sigh. "For the moment, though, everything is calm. At least at the hospital." He motioned to the kitchen, where Sophie still seemed to be struggling with getting words onto her paper.

"Soph?" Tessa asked. "Is everything okay, sweetie? We have to leave soon." She walked over to where her daughter sat. "What are you working on?"

"I'm trying to come up with a list of questions and things I want to ask Scott. Last time, I was so nervous, he did most of the talking, so I never really got a chance to ask him anything. I'm afraid if I don't write it down, I'm going to get nervous again and forget everything."

"That's a good idea," Tessa said, looking over to the paper. There were some basic questions like if he had any pets, what he liked to watch on television, and his favorite color … the usual stuff a seven year would old ask. After that, the paper was filled with grey smudges from questions written and erased. Clearly her daughter was struggling. It wasn't hard for Tessa to figure out why. "Can I help you?"

Sophie looked up at her mother with sad eyes and nodded.

"Well, whenever you used to ask me about Scott, you always wanted to know why he wasn't around like all of the others dads were."

"You told me it was because he lived so far away," her daughter replied.

"I did," Tessa said, chewing her bottom lip. Perhaps now was a good time to be a little more direct with her daughter. "But he didn't always," she continued. "He used to live right here in Forest Hills. He left town while I was still pregnant with you."

"Why?" Sophie asked.

"That's an excellent question, and one that perhaps you should add to your list." She pointed to the paper and watched as her daughter wrote, "W*hy did you leave when Mommy was pregnant with me?"*

There were other questions Sophie should ask as well, like why he stayed away so long, and why he chose now to come back, but for the time being, that single question should be sufficient to get the conversation started.

"We should get going," Nicholas said, putting his hand on Tessa's shoulder.

Once at the diner, the three looked around. They were a few minutes early and didn't see Scott yet, so they asked the hostess for two tables next to each other. This time, Tessa wanted to be able to watch Sophie. She especially wanted to see Scott's face when her daughter asked her tough question. It was about time he gave his daughter an explanation for his cowardly disappearing act all those years ago. Twenty minutes later with no sign of Scott, Tessa checked the bus schedule. She supposed it was possible he missed the bus he said he'd be on. The next one was only an hour later. She ordered Sophie a milkshake and tried Scott's number. It went straight to voicemail.

One hour, several more phone and text attempts, and a cheeseburger for each of them later, Tessa, Nicholas, and a very disappointed Sophie left the diner. Tessa took her daughter home, while Nicholas headed to the hospital to check on Ben.

26   HOLLY

Holly sat in the waiting room, hunched over with her head in her hands. Ava, sitting next to her, gently rubbed her back. Ben's father paced the floor, while his mother nervously sat with Holly's own mother, holding her hand in an attempt to comfort her. Holly's father, not one to often show emotion, sat staring straight ahead, a deep sadness in his eyes.

"Holly?" Nicholas asked with a hint of caution, as he approached his sister-in-law.

"Dr. Golden is in with Ben right now," she said, looking up. Red swollen rims framed her glazed over eyes. While she appreciated Ava and Max's hospitality, she did not sleep for even a second. Shutting her eyes only brought her back to the accident. Like an unending loop, the sounds and sights of crushing metal, shattered glass, and excruciating screams played in her mind, torturing her psyche with guilt. She should have waited until they arrived at the cabin to tell Ben such unexpected news. Of course, he'd be distracted. Forcing her eyes to stay open, she felt even worse for leaving her husband's side. What if she missed her final moments with him? Eventually, she got up and paced in her room, haunted by every passing minute. After three torturous hours, she knocked on Ava's door and insisted she drive her back to the hospital. Max stayed back at the house to take care of the kids.

She looked at her brother-in-law. As soon as he heard about Ben's prognosis, he told her about the doctor he knew in the Mid-West. Nicholas had already been so generous with his offer to help pay for the IVF, and now he was offering to help arrange for a top doctor to take over her husband's care. She was overwhelmed with gratitude. "Thank you for bringing him here, Nicholas. I can't tell you how much I appreciate it."

"Of course, Hol. Anything you need ... anything at all. We're here for you."

She nodded with a smile that quickly faded at the sight of Ben's door opening. They all stood as the doctor walked out of the room.

"Nicholas," Dr. Golden said, extending his arm for a handshake. "So nice to see you again."

"It's a pleasure, William, and thank you so much for coming out here on short notice. I hope it wasn't too much of an inconvenience."

"Not at all. My associates are more than capable of handling things at my practice, and I'm way overdue for a visit, although I do wish it were under better circumstances. I must say, however, your brother-in-law has quite the personality."

"So Ben is doing well then?" he asked.

Dr. Golden smiled and looked at Holly. "Is it okay to discuss your husband's condition with your extended family?"

Nodding, Holly took Ava and Nicholas' hands. "Yes, of course, please continue."

He smiled at her and began speaking. "You and your husband were very lucky. In fact, it's remarkable to me you are standing here with only that scratch on your head. The nurse told me you refused treatment, but I imagine you're quite sore today, am I right?"

Holly nodded. After they'd gotten back to Ava's this morning, she let her sister remove the bandage on her forehead and clean up her cut. The bleeding had stopped, and the cut proved to be just a scrape, but a nasty bump along with a bruise appeared. With all of her attention focused on Ben, she hadn't had time to think about herself. Now that the adrenaline was starting to wear off, she had to admit ... her entire body ached.

"I can prescribe you something to take the edge off, but promise me if you have any headaches, trouble with your eyes, or sharp pains, you will let me examine you immediately."

"Okay, thank you," she said, relieved he wasn't also going to pressure her for an exam. She was fine. Well, better than Ben at least. The point was, she needed every possible resource at that hospital to be focused on her husband right now. "So about Ben?" she asked, trying to get the doctor back on track.

"Yes," he said, "as I was saying, he was very lucky. Despite getting banged up the way he did, his brain function seems to be completely normal. I suspect he only has a slight concussion. In fact, he was talking up a storm just now, joking and laughing about how awful your hockey team is doing this year."

"That sounds like Ben," Nicholas said, rolling his eyes, "although really, it's no joking matter."

"But," Holly said, anxious to get past the small talk. It was obvious there was more to this. Nicholas wouldn't have had one of the country's top doctors flown in on a moment's notice just to sit around and shoot the breeze about some crappy hockey team.

"But," Dr. Golden continued, "Ben does have some substantial injuries that will be challenging to treat. We'll keep him in the ICU for now for observation, and then he'll be moved into a private room upstairs.

The good news is he appears to be stable. He's really doing great."

"Oh thank goodness," Ava said. "Isn't that wonderful, Holly?"

"And what's the bad news?" she asked, trying to stay focused. Yes, it was wonderful her husband was getting better, but the doctor started out by saying *the good news is* ... nobody said that unless bad news followed.

"Well, as you know, he had some serious injuries. His right leg shattered and his back took quite a blow, as did his internal organs. None of his vertebrae are broken, however, there is substantial swelling around his spinal cord. As a result, his lower motor functions are impaired."

"Impaired? What are you saying?" Holly asked.

"Well, two things really. My orthopedist is arriving tonight. He'll assess Ben to see if we can fully repair his leg. He'll no doubt need another surgery. However, even if we can reconstruct the bone, there's no guarantee he'll regain use of his legs again."

"So he's paralyzed?" she asked, letting go of the hands she'd been holding to clutch arms instead as the room around her began to sway.

"At the moment, yes. Once the swelling starts to go down, we'll be able to determine the full extent of the injury. Either way, he's looking at a long recovery. I know this is quite a shock, Mrs. Oakes, and I'm sorry."

She paused, giving herself time to take it all in. "You say he's stable, though?" she asked.

Dr. Golden nodded. "Yes."

Closing her eyes, Holly let out a breath and said a silent prayer of thanks. "That's all that matters," she whispered as she wiped the tears going down her face.

27 AVA

Ava left the hospital at Holly's insistence once the doctor gave his report of Ben's improving condition. With Nicholas still there and Tessa on her way, Ava decided it would be all right to leave. After everything that had happened, she wanted some time to spend with her own family, and she'd been worried about Max. Ben was his cousin. She knew he had to be worried sick—they all were. Thankfully, Max didn't have to rush off for another flight that weekend. They'd have a few days together before she'd be on her own again.

As she got into her car, the promotional card for the exhibit, still in the center console of her front seat, caught her eye. *Gregory Douglas, Artist.* She hoped he didn't think she'd purposely blown off the showing last night. Starting her engine, she checked her watch. The gallery was probably just opening for the day. She decided she had time to swing by and drop off a note of apology for Gregory before heading home. She quickly called Max, gave him an update on Ben, and told him she'd be home after making a short stop.

"Hello?" she called out, walking through the door. The last time she'd been there had been several years ago with Tessa. They'd come for an exhibit, but didn't stay long as Tessa ran into a man she *thought* she was dating. However, upon meeting his *wife* that night, she realized he was only looking for some action on the side. Instead of looking at art, they went back to Ben and Holly's place to overindulge in junk food.

Standing in the middle of the room, Ava took a deep breath. There was nothing like the smell of a painting ... nothing.

"Can I help you?" A slender older man, with thinning hair, and wearing glasses that were much too big for his face, walked into the room.

"Oh, hello. My name is Ava. Ava Wallis. I'm an acquaintance of the artist you have on display."

"Mr. Douglas," he replied.

"Yes," she nodded.

"He had quite an opening last night. I don't blame you for coming back. It was a bit crowded, but I hope you had a nice time. Can I show you some of my favorite pieces now that there's room to get up close?"

"Oh," she responded, "actually, I wasn't here last night. I wanted to, but I'm afraid I had a family emergency." She briefly looked around before returning her gaze to the man. "His pieces are lovely, but I really only have a few minutes. Is it possible to leave him a note? I don't want him thinking I was a no-show."

"Certainly," he replied. "Or you can tell him in person. He's coming in now."

Ava turned around as Gregory walked in the door ... his smile once again throwing her off guard.

"So you made it after all," he said, gently placing his hand on her shoulder. "It's nice to see you again."

She tried to ignore the quiver she felt down her spine solely from his touch, convincing herself with a silent breath it meant nothing. At the same time, nerves settled in as she tried to get her words out. She and Max were happy ... solid. They always had been. There was nothing going on here. It was innocent ... *It was the damn smile.* Leaving a note would have been so much easier. "I-I'm so sorry I missed your opening last night. We had a family issue."

"Don't tell me you lost your son again," he teased, his green eyes picking up an extra shimmer from the overhead lights.

"No," she said, a small giggle escaping her lips. She brought her hands up to her face to try to hide her reddening cheeks. "Nothing like that."

"Well good, and I hope everything is okay now. I was worried when you didn't show up. The Ava I remembered was very serious about her art."

His shift from playful to sincere caught her by surprise. "Oh. Thank you," she responded. "I think it will be. Okay that is."

"I was just telling your friend here what a smashing success your show was last night," the man from the gallery said.

Ava smiled at him, grateful for the interjection into what was about to turn into an awkward game of what should we talk about next? At least for her anyway.

"Yes, I heard it was wall to wall people, and from the looks of the open spots on the wall, I'd say you sold quite a few pieces."

"Oh dear," the man exclaimed apologetically, "that part you weren't supposed to notice. A respectable gallery should never have blank wall space. I was just getting ready to fix that."

"Not to worry, Gene. Only Ava would notice that," Gregory told him. "She used to run a premiere gallery out on the West Coast."

"You don't say?" the man replied.

"Oh, well, I don't know about premiere." She felt a blush rising to her cheeks again. "But I did enjoy those days. It was many, many years ago, mind you … feels like several lifetimes ago. Anyway, I really do need to get going."

"I'm in town for a bit while the exhibit runs," Gregory said, once again putting his hand on Ava's shoulder. "If you're not busy, maybe you'd like to come back? We'll be having a reception next Thursday morning for critics. It would be nice to see a friendly face."

Smiling, Ava nodded. Only top artists in the industry had separate critic receptions outside of their openings. She remembered how nerve-racking they could be, both for the artists and the gallery owners. Max would be back at work, and she could take Ryan to the sitter. Why shouldn't she do something for herself once in a while? And she'd tell Max about it. That way, she wouldn't have to feel guilty about doing something behind his back. Not that she was doing anything wrong by coming to the gallery. She'd want to come even if it wasn't for Gregory. No, he had nothing to do with this. "Sure," she responded. "I'd be glad to."

"Great!" he said, clasping his hands together. "Thank you so much, Ava. I'm always a bundle of nerves during these things. It will be so much easier to get through it having you by my side."

"Right," she murmured, once again thrown off by what she hoped was just an innocent comment by an old client.

28 TESSA

"**L**ook, I don't want to hear your excuses. All I know is I sent you money to come out here, more than you probably needed to cover your expenses now that I think about it, and you never showed. Forgetting for a moment the part where you took advantage of my generosity, a very disappointed seven year old sat and waited for you to show up for over an hour."

"What did you tell her?" he asked.

"Well, not what I wanted to," Tessa replied. Tapping her fingers on her desk, she glanced over at the clock. This bozo had already wasted enough of her precious rehearsal time, although she had to admit her actors were pretty amazing. If they had to go on that evening, they'd be impressive without a doubt—she couldn't imagine how spectacular they'd be on opening night. At least one aspect of her life was stress-free.

"I'm so sorry, Tessa," he pleaded. "I promise to make it up to Sophie and to you. I had every intention of coming out, but at the last minute I got a call for a job interview. I couldn't turn it down."

"On a Saturday? And you could have called. You knew she'd be sitting there waiting for you." *You knew she'd been waiting for you for seven years.*

"Everything happened so fast, and I didn't have a chance to get in touch with you. I feel terrible. Ever since I connected with Sophie my entire outlook has changed. I've made so many mistakes with my life, Tess. I know my apology probably means nothing to you, but I am so sorry. I truly wish I could turn back time and change the past. While we both know that's not possible, I have to do something ... for Sophie. I'm trying to be a better person, and that starts with securing a stable job. It's not too late to be a father to my daughter. I intend to be there for her going forward—to make up for lost time. She's my everything now, and I was hoping you'd give me another chance to see her.

Tessa closed her eyes. *The smooth talker. I love you, Tessa. I'm going to be there for you. You're my everything.* The words flooded her brain as if they'd taken place yesterday, and not the day Scott proposed to her all those years ago.

"So did you get the job?" she asked, a cold chill wrapping around her voice. While his apologies might work on Sophie, they meant nothing to her.

"No. Not that job. I found something even better. I meet with the owner on Thursday ... only—"

"Only?" she asked. *What now?*

"Well, I hate to ask this, but it's for a really good job ... a sales manager in an established company. It's perfect for me given my education and experience. The owner says the job is mine, I just need to go meet with him in person. This is just the break I've been waiting for."

"Just what is your experience, Scott?" Exactly what had kept her ex-fiancé busy these past years?

"Sales. I can be convincing when I need to be," he responded.

No kidding.

"I'm ready to move up into the world. Management is where all of the big bucks are. The problem is the job's out of state."

"Why's that a problem?" she asked. It's not like he was tied down to where he currently lived.

"Well, it's like I told you last week, I'm a little short on funds."

Shaking her head, she sighed. So that's what he wanted. "You're asking me for more money? What happened to all the money I sent you already?"

"I had to buy a suit for the interview ... and I'm a little behind on some of my bills. Don't worry, once I get this job, I promise to pay every penny back. With interest if you want. It pays six-figures. I just need a little help getting over this hump. I promise this is the last time."

"You said the job was yours. Does that mean they made you an offer?" Before she agreed to send him money again, she wanted to get her facts straight.

"Yeah, yeah. It's a done deal. I just have to go talk to them, but I need help getting there. I have to fly, and the tickets are a fortune."

She crinkled her forehead. None of this made sense. "If they want you so badly, shouldn't they be paying all your expenses?"

"They're going to reimburse me, but with the way security is at the airlines these days, I have to pay for everything myself. How's weekend after next, once I'm settled?"

Her head was still stuck on the airline stuff. Was that true? She knew security at airports was no joking matter these days. When she and Nicholas flew they had to show their ID about twenty times before they were allowed to board. She supposed she could call Max—he worked for the airlines—but could she risk Nicholas finding out? Damn, she hated keeping secrets from her husband. As generous as he was, even he had his limits, and Tessa was almost certain sending money to Scott was one of them. However, now wasn't the time for her to try to figure that out. Sophie's well-being was the only thing that mattered. Her daughter deserved at least one more visit with the man that fathered her, at the very least, to have her questions answered. After that, he could go to hell, for all Tessa cared.

Her silence no doubt concerned Scott. "Please, Tessa, I promise this is the last time. If I pass up this opportunity, I'm back to square one. I want Sophie to be able to tell her friends that her daddy is a big shot manager. I want my little girl to be proud of me."

Her daughter's hopeful eyes stared at her through the picture frame perched on her desk as the recent events from school re-surfaced. *The family tree art project. The kids teasing her about her real dad. How sad her Ava and Holly said she was that night. How it all could have been different if she knew her dad and was proud of him. Sophie.* Wasn't she what this was all about?

"How much do you need?"

29   HOLLY

Holly held her husband's hand as she patiently waited for him to open his eyes. It seemed she was doing a lot of that lately. This time however, Dr. Golden had assured her it was normal and to be expected. His orthopedic team had just finished their surgery on his leg.

"He's practically bionic," they teased as they wheeled him back into his room. "We usually say good as new, but in his case, he's better than new. Now we just have to see if his spinal cord can work its magic to give him mobility."

Dr. Golden excused himself to take a phone call, leaving her alone in the room with the nurse and the surgeon, who continued to check Ben's vitals. Was that normal protocol? Did the surgeon always stay with the patient after the procedure was complete? Probably not, she reasoned, but in this case, the surgeon was called in only to take care of Ben. One more thing she'd have to remember to thank Nicholas for. The sting of tears overtook her as she thought of the moment the emergency room doctor had told her to say good-bye to her husband. What if they hadn't been able to save him? No. She couldn't let her thoughts go there. *What if* no longer mattered. Moving her lips across Ben's face, she could feel his breath upon her cheek. It was the best feeling in the world ... she had so much to be grateful for.

"So it's a waiting game from here?" she asked, positioning herself back into her seat, still holding his hand.

"Not entirely," the surgeon responded. "He has a lot of rehab work ahead of him and is going to need a tremendous amount of support and patience. You will also. It's often said that rehab is harder on the family than on the patient. However, from the entourage I've seen coming in and out, it looks like you've got the support side covered."

"Yes," she nodded, "I'm very lucky."

"To have married me?" the hoarse voice asked as eyes fluttered open. "I agree. Some vacation we're having, huh?" He coughed as he struggled to continue. "Sorry, they don't have room at the inn here for you, too, babe. But I'll save the pudding for you at my next meal. Only the best for my sweetie."

"I see our resident jokester is waking up," Dr. Golden said, walking into the room. "Ben, how are you feeling?"

"Awesome." He cleared his throat again as the nurse began checking his stats. "What time are the wheelchair races? I heard they just waxed the sixth floor."

"I'll have to check on that and get back to you," Dr. Golden responded, shaking his head with a snicker. "Holly, have you met Ben's surgeon, Dr. Steiner?"

"Not officially. It's nice to meet you," she replied, only nodding as she didn't want to let go of Ben to shake his hand. She immediately turned back to her husband. "Sweetie, are you sure you're okay? They can give you something if you're in pain. You don't have to be a martyr."

"I can't feel a damn thing. I take it that's not good, Doc," he said, his voice taking a more serious tone."

"Nah, I wouldn't worry about it," the doctor told him. "You've got quite a bit of morphine pumping through you at the moment."

"Another perk of this luxury resort?" Ben asked.

"Something like that," he said, laughing. Dr. Steiner closed up Ben's chart and looked up with encouraging eyes. "Your vitals are remarkably strong for what you've been through, but it's important you get your rest today. We'll want to get you started on an aggressive program of therapy as soon as you're ready. By the looks of things, I'd say that could start as early as the end of the week. Do you have any questions for me?"

"My surgery, it was successful?" he asked.

Holly looked away, knowing her husband so well. She knew exactly what he wanted to know; the one thing no one could truly answer.

"In terms of repairing the damage to your leg? Yes."

He took a deep breath, so obviously trying to come to terms with the possible answer to his next question. Holly felt the grip around her hand tighten. His hands worked, why didn't his legs? "So then I'll walk again, right?" he asked quietly.

Dr. Steiner pursed his lips together and hugged the chart close to his body. "That's certainly our goal."

"But—"

"There are no guarantees," Dr. Golden interjected. "As we discussed the other day, spinal cord swelling can sometimes mask permanent damage."

"Right," he said, looking completely defeated. His hand dropped from Holly's and fell to the side of the bed.

"Ben," the doctor continued, "I want you to keep something in mind throughout your therapy. The brain is a remarkable and complex organ. The more we study it, the more we learn about the connection between positive thinking and positive outcomes. I know it sounds like a bunch of new age crap, but right now, when your body is fighting so hard to heal, now is not the time to give up. Do you hear me?"

Ben nodded, looking about as convinced as Holly's fifth grade students on the first day of school when she tried to tell them how much fun they were going to have in her math class.

Dr. Golden, completely in tune to his patient's reaction, continued. "Now I want you to look at your wife. Look her straight in the eyes and tell her you're not giving up. Tell her you know it will be hard. Tell her it might take longer than you'd want, and yes, tell her it's probably going to hurt like hell. But you look her in the eyes, the woman you promised to love for better or for worse, and you tell her that you, Benjamin Oakes, will not give up."

Ben waited while Holly wiped her tears away and put his trembling hand out for her to hold once more. "I promise, Holly," he began, his voice still sounding groggy from being under anesthesia, "for you … for us, and for the family we *will* have one day. I promise not to give up. I'm going to fight through this. However long it takes, and for as hard and painful as it might be. For better or for worse. I will not give up."

The determination in his eyes matched the words that left his lips. Nodding, Holly met his gaze and replied, "I'm going to hold you to that promise, Benjamin Oakes, and I promise to be by your side the entire way."

30 AVA

Ava clenched her teeth almost as tightly as she gripped the wheel on her drive over to the gallery. She shouldn't have snapped at Ryan's babysitter like that when she'd dropped her son off. Mrs. Connelly had only made an innocent and polite comment as to how pretty she looked all dressed up and with makeup on. She was completely annoyed she was letting her nerves get the best of her. She would look this way for any important *business* meeting, not that Mrs. Connelly would have assumed otherwise. Perhaps the bright red lipstick was a poor choice.

At least she'd been honest with Max as he left for work ... she told him she'd be spending the morning looking at art. It wasn't her fault he didn't ask where or with whom ... or make any comments as to her appearance. A husband should be more interested in his wife's activities and how she spent her day. She always took the time to ask him details about his flights.

Pulling into the parking lot, she regretted being so early. There were only two cars there. No doubt Gregory and Gene, the owner of the gallery. Why did she agree to this again? The art. Right. *Concentrate on the art.* Just that thought alone brought a smile to her face. She wondered if she'd know any of the critics. It'd been years of course, but back in the day she'd known them all and was a pro at wooing them. Suddenly, the rush she'd missed so much returned as she wiped off her lipstick and headed toward the building.

"Ava!" Gregory called, pouncing on her with a hug the moment she walked through the door like a needy child. "Thank God you're here. I'm a wreck."

"You're going to be fine." She pulled away under the auspices of having to take off her coat. "You're a seasoned pro." Her confidence, having finally returned just moments ago in the parking lot, started to slip again the moment his strong arms embraced her. She needed a Plan B: distance. "How about some coffee?" she asked, already walking over to the table where drinks were set up. If his hands had something *in them*, he couldn't put them *on her*.

"Oh, no, thank you," he insisted, walking toward her. "I'm already shaky enough as it is."

Taking a few steps back, she nodded. "Maybe some herbal tea, instead?" The corners of her lips formed a slight smile.

"Champagne would be better, but I suppose it's a bit early for that. Anyway, how does everything look? Gene filled in all those blank spaces you noted last time you were here with some more of my pieces. Come to think of it, you haven't actually had a chance to see my exhibit yet, have you?"

"No, not yet," she answered, looking around, but more to figure out where Gene was than to check out the art. Being alone with Gregory was not part of her Plan B. However, he was right. She did want to see the exhibit. Now was as good of a time as any. It would keep her moving at the very least. She walked from piece to piece and was grateful Gregory stayed by the front windows, allowing her to take a moment to herself to enjoy the true reason for her visit. Circling back toward him, she smiled. "Lovely," she said, cautious with her words. He was incredibly talented, but now was not the time to gush. "The critics will love it."

"And the arrangement?"

Standing back to take in the entire scene, she tilted her head—a habit she had picked up from her early days interning at the prestigious Main Street Gallery back in her college days. Her mentor, Cynthia Sims, used to joke that perhaps by tilting, she was combining both sides of her brain into one, to bring in more clarity. Whatever the reason, it seemed to work.

"Well, it looks fine the way it is," she started, "but—"

"But if it were your gallery you'd do something different?" Gene asked, entering the room without warning from a back area.

"I'm so sorry." Ava was quick to apologize, a cold sweat taking over her entire body. If she could think of an excuse to run out the door that very minute, she would in record speed. "Everything looks great, really."

"Please." Kindness and sincerity filled Gene's voice. "My reputation is on the line here today, too. If you have suggestions, I do want to hear them. Sometimes a fresh pair of eyes is needed."

"Well ..." Ava, who truly hoped she wasn't overstepping her bounds, walked around the room one more time to double check her observations. "The three lights you have above this wall of paintings are casting a shadow that's distracting. I think if you adjust them slightly up so they're bouncing just above the paintings instead of directly on them, they'll highlight the brushstrokes nicely."

She waited for Gene's reaction before going on, remembering Cynthia's initial reaction when she'd first recommended adjusting a light fixture during her internship interview. At first, Ms. Sims, tops in her industry, became defensive. However, upon trying the preposterous suggestion, Ava found herself being offered the highly sought after position on the spot.

"Yes," Gene murmured, rubbing his chin. "I didn't notice that before. It's so subtle, and yet, I think you're absolutely right. Brilliant."

"Anything else, Ava?" Gregory asked, grinning.

She stopped at a collection of three paintings tucked in a corner. "The colors here are so vibrant and fresh. To me they're exactly what you need to set the tone for the day. If this were my gallery, I'd want my customers to see these first. They should be your showcase pieces. Let's get those critics in a good mood from the moment they walk in the door."

"Absolutely," Gene exclaimed, already removing the painting he'd chosen to leave the first impression, for the much more suitable works Ava picked. He let her arrange the paintings as she saw fit and reached for a stepladder, which was hidden behind a faux wall to work on the lighting.

"She's amazing, isn't she?" Gregory asked, as Gene made the adjustments.

Ava took a step back and watched the shadows disappear, just as she had envisioned they would.

"Just fabulous," he agreed. Putting the ladder away, he checked his watch. "Everyone should be arriving soon. Would you excuse me for a moment? I forgot to put out the pastries I picked up this morning. No one ever eats them, mind you, but it you don't have them available, you never hear the end of it.

Well, I'm sure you know how it is, Ava. I'll be right back."

"You don't think he's upset, do you?" Ava asked once she was alone with Gregory. "I mean about me giving him advice about his set up."

"Gene?" he asked. "Oh, no. I've known him for years. He's a great guy, but his exhibits all look the same. I think he really appreciated your take on things. I know I did. You're something else."

Before Ava had a chance to remember Plan B, Gregory wrapped his arm around her waist, pulling her in close to his body. She allowed herself to give in to the movement and stared into his eyes, getting lost in the moment as their lips slowly inched closer together, his breath warm against her skin. *Was this really happening?* With just barely enough room to let air pass between them, she pushed her hands against his shoulders.

"No," she said with determination. "This is not why I came here today."

"*Ava, wait! I'm sorry,*" was the last thing she heard as she ran out the door.

31 TESSA

"I want you to know I'm not mad at you, sweetheart, but I am concerned." Nicholas took a seat next to his wife in the audience of the theater as she watched her actors run through the production from start to finish. Opening night was quickly approaching, and she couldn't be happier with how everything was pulling together. From media coverage to ticket sales, the business side was a well-oiled machine, thanks to her husband. And as far as the show went … well, in her humble and professional opinion, it was in the same caliber as Broadway. Make that Broadway on a budget … a very small budget.

"Concerned?" she whispered, not wanting to interrupt the scene. Had she spent too much on set design and costumes? The ballroom scene was a bit elaborate, but in her defense, it wasn't easy recreating a twentieth-century gilded mansion on the cheap.

"Yes," he continued in a low voice, his view focused on the stage. "The bank called me last week. I had to give approval for a $5,000 wire to an account owned by an S. Warren in Oxford. That's Scott, correct?"

Her eyes widened, not at all expecting that response. "Take five!" she yelled up to her crew. *The bank called Nicholas?* They didn't mention anything about needing approval when she put in the wire request. Beads of sweat along her hairline began to form as she thought of an excuse to tell her husband.

"It's okay, sweetheart. I told them it was fine. I know you'd do anything to help and protect Sophie. I just wish you'd come to me first."

Turning her head to her husband, she honestly didn't know how to respond. "I'm so sorry, Nicholas. You're right, I should have told you. I was afraid you'd say no, and I didn't want to disappoint Sophie. Well, he got laid off and was low on cash. At first I only sent him a smaller amount to cover travel expenses to get to Sophie, but then he was offered this great job out of state and needed more money to travel there and help cover some bills. He kept telling me what a great opportunity it was and how he only wanted Sophie to be proud of him." She paused, hoping Nicholas understood why she had made the decision to send the wire behind his back, and added, "It's just I remember what it was like to be struggling and down on your luck."

"You mean when he deserted you and didn't help pay for any of his child's expenses?" Nicholas reminded her.

Hanging her head down low, Tessa nodded. As much as it stung, her husband spoke the truth. Scott had never paid her a dime of child support. He had no clue how she scraped and struggled. Even an extra fifty dollars a month would have seemed like a fortune to her. "He promised to pay us back," she said, trying to rationalize her actions. "His job is in management. It sounds like he'll be high up in the company."

Nicholas put his arm around Tessa and pulled her in to give her a kiss. "You're such a kind and trusting soul. It's one of the things I love most about you. Unfortunately, I've been around enough shady people over the years to know when something doesn't sound quite right."

"So you don't believe him?"

"Not for a second. When he bailed on us at the diner, I'll admit I was a little suspicious. I decided to give him the benefit of the doubt … for Sophie's sake. However, as soon as the bank called me, I knew he was scheming. I figured he had to have had to come up with a pretty strong story to convince you to give him that kind of money. After all, you're one shrewd business woman yourself."

"You just said I was kind and trusting."

"Yes," he said, laughing "but in a smart way."

"I'm not feeling smart at the moment. I'm also wondering why you approved the wire." Did she miss something here? Since when did her husband hand out large sums of cash to cons?

"Well, I didn't want to be the guy who wouldn't give money to Sophie's father. She'd never forgive or believe me that he was up to something. Not without proof at least. So, I hired a private investigator. I was curious to see why exactly Mr. Scott Warren needed five thousand of our dollars. I may be wealthy, but that money is still hard earned."

Sighing, Tessa looked at her husband. She wanted to know as well, but at the same time, she dreaded the answer. "I'm now guessing it wasn't so he could make travel arrangements to meet his new boss?"

"I'm really sorry, sweetheart." Reaching into his briefcase, Nicholas pulled out a folder of photos and handed them to her. "These arrived this morning from my investigator."

She examined each one carefully: Scott dressed in cheesy looking designer-wanna-be clothes ... Scott getting into an older model sports car with a scantily-clad blonde ... Scott and the blonde arriving at a bank ... Scott leaving the bank, shoving a wad of cash in his jacket pocket with the blonde trying to keep up behind him in her five-inch heels ... Scott and his blonde in what looked like a fancy restaurant, sipping champagne.

"Would it be too much to hope this is a celebratory dinner in honor of his new job?" Tessa asked, already knowing the answer.

"Sorry. According to the investigator's report, Scott also purchased a flat screen television that afternoon. He paid for it with cash. And, as it turns out, he's not unemployed. He's in sales ... been working for the same company for the last six years. He never left town or intended to leave town. He and his blonde continued to party all weekend ... on our tab."

That asshole. Tessa was stunned. She'd believed every word of his story. The same way she'd believed everything he'd promised her back in college when she was pregnant with Sophie. She should've known better. He'd taken advantage of her ... of Nicholas really. That creep saw she'd married into money and came to get one thing and one thing only: a cut of Nicholas' fortune. How long did he really think he could keep it up until she'd catch on? It was obvious he had no interest in Sophie whatsoever. What was he going to ask for next? Ten thousand? Didn't he think they'd figure it out eventually?

"So now what? Do we call the police? He clearly has no intentions of repaying us." As she contemplated the financial aspects, she realized they had an even bigger problem on their hands. "Nicholas, what are we going to tell Sophie when Scott comes to town next weekend? If he comes to town next weekend. She's going to be devastated." Tessa closed her eyes. Once again Scott had managed to turn all of their lives completely upside down. Only this time, a little girl's feelings were at stake.

"Don't worry, my love," Nicholas said, with his usual charming and calming smile. "I've already got it all figured out."

32 AVA

"**I** love you." Ava twirled her hair in her fingers as she said the words into the phone, a habit she'd had for years.

"I love you, too, babe. Are you sure everything is okay?" Max asked.

After the scene with Gregory at the gallery, Ava jumped in her car and drove directly home. She wanted to call her sisters, but Holly … well, she had enough to deal with, and Tessa was no doubt completely immersed in her own stress what with her opening night quickly approaching. Instead, she paced her living room, re-playing the events of the morning. *I did nothing wrong. Our lips never touched.* Still, it bothered her that she hesitated when Gregory grabbed her. She should have immediately pushed away. Instead, she let him hold her until just before that moment when their lips were about to touch. *But they never did.* Stopping to look at her face in the foyer mirror, she pulled her fingers out of the curls she created. Where those wrinkles above her eyebrows there yesterday? She tried to smooth them out with her fingers.

"Ava? Are you there?" Max asked. "You're acting strange. I'm a little worried. Do you need me to come home? I could try to switch flights with someone. Maybe I can come home tonight instead of tomorrow."

"No, I'm fine, really." Was she acting strange? The last thing she needed was for Max to worry about her. He was already worried enough about Ben. What she really wanted was for everything to just go back to normal. "I was just thinking about … what to make for dinner. I forgot to take something out of the freezer this morning." In a way it was true. Looked like they'd be ordering pizza again. "Anyway, I'll figure something out. Everything's fine."

"Well, okay. Listen, babe. I want to apologize."

"For what?" she asked, walking into the kitchen to get a drink. Now he was the one acting strange. "You don't have anything to be sorry for."

"I do," he said. "Ben's accident was a wakeup call for me. I'm just sorry it had to happen for me to realize."

"Realize?" She opened her bottle of water. Just the other day, she'd read about a woman who eliminated all wrinkles on her face just by upping her daily water intake.

"Yes," he continued, "that I've been selfish."

"No, honey. You're not selfish. You work really hard to support this family. We all understand that."

"Ava, do you remember how we met?"

She bit her bottom lip and laughed silently. She hadn't thought about that day for years, although it had been quite memorable. "You were the nude model for my art class. Kind of hard to forget something like that. I couldn't look away from you, to be honest."

"Ah-ha! So you *were* gawking! I knew it."

"Okay, well, maybe a little," she giggled. "Anyway, what does that have to do with you being selfish?"

"That day, I noticed you because of the passion in your eyes. Although I'd wished it were due to me standing there naked in front of you, I knew it was because you were completely in your element ... surrounded by art. You gave all of that up to raise a family. *Our family.*"

"We made the decision together, Max. I don't regret it at all."

"I know that, babe. But that doesn't change the fact that you gave up your dream ... for us ... for me. I shouldn't have been so quick to say no when you wanted to go to the gallery the night of Ben's accident, especially when it was something so important to you."

"Oh, it's okay. You were tired."

"No," he continued, "it's not okay at all. And I want to make it up to you. We should go tomorrow when I get home. I know it's not the same as an opening, but we can still make a date night out of it. You know—get dressed up, grab some dinner."

"Tomorrow?" Ava asked. Panic rose in her throat. Gregory's exhibit would still be running. He was the last person she wanted to see, and she certainly didn't want him and Max in the same room together. She had visions of Gregory apologizing to her in front of her husband.

"So sorry for making a pass at you, Ava. Oh, is this your husband? Very nice to meet you. Well, enjoy the exhibit."

Ridiculous notion, no doubt, but her thoughts weren't exactly altogether rational at the moment.

"We can't go tomorrow," she blurted out as her nervous pacing to the living room and back picked up again.

"Why?" Max asked.

Crap. She was unprepared for that question. "Well … um … you know I don't like to talk bad about exhibits, but I stopped in the other day. The owner was lovely, but I wasn't impressed with the artist's work at all, and he still has another two weeks for his run. I say we wait for it to clear out and then head over. It will be much more enjoyable."

"Okay, if that's what you want, babe. You know about these things better than I do. Are you sure? Didn't you say the artist was your friend?" he asked.

"Well an old client, but that's my point. You know how bad my game face is. It would be so awkward."

"Yeah, it is pretty awful," he agreed. "Okay, then we'll wait. But we're definitely going soon. I insist."

"I really appreciate you doing this, Max." She caught a glimpse of her smile in the mirror as she walked by once more and paused. For the first time all day, the overwhelming feeling of nervous gloom no longer clouded her mind. Funny how a simple gesture by one person could change her mood so dramatically. Maybe it was because he was the person she needed it from the most. He always did have perfect timing.

33 TESSA

They took their seats in the diner and waited once again for Scott to appear.

"Do you think he'll show this time?" Tessa whispered to Nicholas from the next table while Sophie sat in her booth, fidgeting with her paper of questions as she watched the door.

"I think so. In his mind, he needs to play it cool. It's the only way to keep you and Sophie happy, which in turn will keep the funds flowing. If he bolted now, it would just make him look more suspicious," Nicholas replied.

"He's here!" Sophie shrieked as the door to the restaurant swung open.

All three of them rose to their feet as Scott approached. Nicholas seemed so calm and collected, while Tessa was a furious mess. She wanted to reach out and wring Scott's neck, but she had promised her husband she'd stay composed and follow his lead. She trusted him completely and knew he had Sophie's best interests at heart.

"There she is," Scott said, approaching Sophie with arms wide open, "the prettiest girl in all of Forest Hills."

Tessa watched with interest as her daughter looked not to her for approval, but to Nicholas, who gave her a nod, before she gave Scott a quick hug, then pulled away.

"Where were you last time? You were supposed to be here," Sophie told him, crinkling her brow.

Tessa couldn't help but crack her lips into the tiniest of smile. Her daughter's shy nervousness had apparently been replaced by her spunky attitude, that's for sure. *Get ready, Scott, that's just the warm up question. The real kicker is still to come.*

"Oh, well I, um, I had a job interview. Didn't your mom tell you?"

"But we waited and waited. Why didn't you call to tell us?" she asked, obviously not satisfied with the answer he'd given.

He looked at Tessa with pleading eyes, probably hoping she'd chime in and offer help in the explanation department. He was sorely mistaken.

Instead she said, "Sweetie, Nicholas and I will be sitting right here at the next table if you need anything."

"Okay, Mommy."

This time there would be no barriers. Nicholas and Tessa both wanted and needed to see and hear everything. As Sophie and Scott settled into the booth, the conversation turned away from his disappearing act and more into idle chit-chat. Once again Scott was asking the questions, mostly about school and friends. Tessa realized it was all planned on his part. As long as he kept control of the conversation, Sophie couldn't ask uncomfortable questions. Well, he wasn't getting off that easily. After the waitress brought their requested food and drinks, Tessa caught her daughter's eye and motioned to her paper. She gave a reassuring smile and nodded.

Sophie waited until Scott put a forkful of eggs in his mouth and asked, "Why *did* you leave when Mommy was pregnant with me?"

Without warning, eggs flew out and across the table as he signaled to the waitress for water to help ease his ensuing coughing fit. To save time and to keep him from procrastinating, Nicholas handed him his water instead.

"I believe Sophie's waiting for an answer," he said as he sat back down with Tessa, once Scott finished wiping his mouth. "In fact, I believe my wife deserves an explanation as well."

It wasn't how she had expected the conversation to go. Her intention was to allow Sophie privacy on the matter, but she appreciated her husband's boldness. And now that she thought of it, Scott would probably be less inclined to give a bogus and vague response knowing there were three pairs of eyes and ears on him, two of which would not put up with his bullshit. Scratch that. Make that three pairs that wouldn't put up with his bullshit. The look on Sophie's face told Tessa she was all business. Perhaps her daughter had picked up on Scott's true personality after all.

"Oh ... well ... I ..." Scott nervously looked around at his audience. Surely he'd expected this question at some point and had something prepared. "I didn't leave, Sophie, not really. You're always with me in my heart every single day. Right here," he said, forming a fist and tapping it over his chest, "where it matters."

Tessa looked down to keep Sophie from seeing her disgusted look and rolling eyes. *Was he serious?* There was no way her daughter would fall for that crap.

"That doesn't make sense," she responded. "My mommy says I'm always with her in her heart *and* we live together, so I still don't get why you left."

Good girl, Soph. Make him squirm.

"It's ... complicated, but I honestly never meant to hurt you—or your mom. And I wanted to come back, Sophie, I really did, but with work, it was difficult for me to get away."

Complicated. Was that the best he could do?

"My Nicholas works really hard, and he always comes back, even when he has to go on business trips. Back in September he came home early to take me to the father/daughter dance. And he's been to all of my piano recitals. He *always* shows up when he promises to, and he *never* lets me down."

Yay, Sophie!

"Well you're a very lucky girl," Scott said, taking the final gulp of his coffee before standing up. "Anyway, it was great to see everyone again."

"You're leaving?" Tessa asked, surprised. Apparently his ego could no longer take the lecture by the seven year old.

"Yes," he replied. "I start my new job soon, and I need to wrap up some last minute things back home to get ready for my move. My bus will be here shortly." Grabbing his jacket he turned toward his daughter. "Sophie?"

"Yeah?" she asked, barely looking up. Scott stood with open arms—the same way he'd greeted her earlier. Slowly getting out of her seat, she kept her distance and only mumbled, "Bye."

"I'll be in touch," he said to Tessa and Nicholas has he headed toward the door.

"Wait up," Nicholas called, grabbing the briefcase he'd brought in with him. He followed Scott out to the parking lot.

"Are you okay?" Tessa asked, lifting her up and onto her lap.

"Yes," she said, "but if it's okay with you, I don't think I want to see Scott again." Tears streamed down her face as Tessa held her tight.

"You don't have to do anything you don't want to do, sweetheart," she said, rubbing her back in small circles.

"Mommy?"

"Yes, sweetie?" She looked at her daughter's tear-streaked face.

"I wish Nicholas was my real dad."

Tessa smiled as she pushed her hair out of her eyes. "He already is, sweetheart. He already is."

34 HOLLY

"Take me back." Ben sat on the exam table, staring straight ahead. His physical therapist, Marc, had just spent the last twenty minutes massaging his legs to keep his muscles from weakening. Ben hadn't felt any of it—not the pushing, not the kneading, not even the pinches Holly knew Marc had thrown in to test him. Nothing. Holly stood by Ben's side the entire time waiting for any sign from her husband … even the tiniest flinch to let her know a sensation of some sort had reached his brain. But as was the case each day, twice a day, for what felt like forever, there was nothing.

"Babe, you still have an hour to go. You haven't even started your exercises yet," she reminded him.

"Exercises?" he said louder than Holly would have liked. He'd been in a foul mood all day, ever since his morning therapy session when he insisted on trying to *walk* assisted by parallel bars, despite Marc's contention he was pushing himself too hard and setting himself up for disappointment. *That was an understatement.* As predicted, his legs wouldn't move on their own. He'd been sulking all day over it. The other patients in the rehab room, upon hearing his outburst, turned to look at Ben. "Exercises?" he repeated, this time softer. "That's a joke. Hol, I'm not doing anything. Every day since this cast has come off has been the same. I lie still like the slug I've become, and Marc here moves my leg up and down and sideways. How is that *me* exercising?"

"It's exercising your spine and reminding your brain, so when movement does return, you'll have an easier time getting back on your feet," Marc told him.

"You mean if," Ben corrected. "And so far, that *if* seems to be a more likely *not going to ever happen.* The accident was quite a while ago."

"Your recovery is up to you," Marc began. "The mind—"

"Yeah, yeah," he said, smirking. "Dr. Golden told me all about that hocus pocus mind crap. If it were true, I'd be walking by now."

"I'm really sorry, Marc," Holly said, giving her husband a nasty look. "He's just having a rough day."

"No worries, Mrs. Oakes, I'm used to it. Actually, Ben," he said, bringing his face directly in front of his patient's, "you know what? You're probably right. This is all useless. You should just go back to your room now. I have other patients I could be helping who actually give a damn about their recovery."

Holly stood next to the two men, completely speechless. *Marc was kidding, right? This was some kind of mind game psycho-babble people did when they wanted to get you to do the opposite of what you want to do. Wasn't it?*

"What?" Ben asked, looking at Marc then Holly. "What about my therapy?"

"It's a waste of time. You said so yourself. In fact, you should probably just go home. There's a waitlist here for rehab rooms, and they're supposed to be filled by patients who will benefit from our services."

"You're not supposed to say that," Ben told him, his tone straining with a level of fear and concern Holly had never heard in her husband's voice before.

She wanted to tell Ben everything would be okay. That Marc was only kidding, that Marc was only saying these things because he was trying to get him to continue his therapy, but the truth was, she wasn't a hundred percent sure that was correct. What if Marc, through his therapy sessions with her husband, had come to the conclusion that Ben really wasn't ever going to be able to walk again?

"Who's going to help me get my mobility back?" he continued, a gruff edge now adding in to the mix of his fear and concern.

"Well, nobody. But it's okay because you've already decided you won't be walking again. So here," Marc pushed his wheelchair right next to the table where Ben sat, "good luck to you, pal. I'll go get your discharge papers started." He patted him on the shoulder and began to leave the room.

"Wait!" Ben called out.

Holly caught a glimpse of a fleeting smile cross Marc's lips as he stopped at the doorway just before he turned back around with his previous stoic expression.

It was all a ploy. She let out a long, silent breath, realizing everything would be okay.

"Yes?" Marc asked.

"I need help getting back into my chair."

Defeat swept over Holly. Was Ben really so stubborn that he'd rather be crippled? What about the promise he had made to her in front of Dr. Golden?

"You have two arms that work just fine," he replied. "You're going to have learn how to use them to get yourself in and out of that chair on your own if this is the life you're choosing. There's not always going to be someone around offering to help you, you know."

Shaking his head, Ben's scowl deepened. "Hol," he said, his frustration growing. He held out his hand. "Do you mind? I just need to hold on to you for balance."

She studied her husband as he sat there looking completely helpless. As much as it pained her, she looked straight back at him and said, "No."

"Excuse me?" he asked. "Hol, I need help."

"I know, that's why we have Marc. To help you with the therapy you promised you would endure. Remember? *For as long as it took, for as difficult as it would be, for not only you, but for us? For better or for worse.* He's here to help you."

Ben put his head back down and sighed. "And you promised to support me when I needed help."

"I'm trying to help you, babe," she said, the all too familiar sting of tears starting to well in her eyes. "Can't you see that? Twenty-four/seven since the accident, all I've done is try to help you." She knew he was speaking out of frustration, but it didn't make his words hurt any less.

"Forget it, I'll do it myself." Sliding his body sideways to line up perfectly next to the chair, he let out a loud grunt and struggled as he attempted to lift his body up and into the seat. Marc caught him before he fell to the floor and put him back on the table.

"Shit," Ben whispered, a single tear now making its way down his cheek.

"It's okay, babe." Holly immediately ran to his side. "I'll help you."

"Here's what I propose," Marc said, looking Ben squarely in the eyes. "We'll work on your arm strength *and* the proper way to get in and out of the chair. In exchange, you'll keep your end of your promise to your wife and let me work on your legs. Deal?"

"I'm sorry." Ben reached out to hold Holly's hand. "Babe, I'm so, so sorry. I didn't mean ... you've been there for me every minute. You didn't deserve ... you don't deserve—"

"I know. It's okay," she replied, resting her head on his shoulder.

"It's easy to let your frustrations get the best of you," Marc told him, "especially when you've been trying to work through this for as long as you have. But you need to trust me, Dr. Golden, your wife, and most of all yourself. They tell me you survived an accident you weren't supposed to survive. That was the hard part. This part is easy, and like you said, I'm really the one doing all the work."

Nodding, Ben squeezed Holly's hand even tighter. "Okay." He gave a determined nod. "You have a deal. Now let's get to work."

35 TESSA

Tessa paced nervously backstage as people raced around her: actors, hair, makeup, costumes, sets, sound, lighting. Every last detail had its own *person* on his or her own mission. It was a controlled chaos, but chaos nonetheless.

"Sweetheart," Nicholas said, guiding her to the back room they'd set up as a post-production lounge, "everything is going to be perfect tonight. The cast is more than prepared, as is the crew. You've got a sellout crowd. There's nothing left for you to do but shine. You, my love, have worked harder than anyone I know to get to where you are today. I couldn't be prouder. Tonight is going to be a night to remember, with much to celebrate."

"He's right," Ava said, already in the room, waiting to give her sister a hug. "I know you need to get back out there, but I asked Nicholas to steal you away for a few minutes so I could see you. Here, these are for you."

The bouquet of roses her older sister thrust toward her were bigger than the size of her own head. "Av," she said, trying to wrap her arms around all of the stems, "thank you. But you're supposed to wait until after the show to give flowers. It's one of those weird superstitious theater things."

"Like *break a leg?* By the way, Tessa, I don't think we should be saying that in front of Holly and Ben."

"Ah, good point," she agreed. "I hadn't thought of that."

"Speaking of," Nicholas said, "I'm going to make sure Ben is set up okay. We have a spot cleared in the front row for his wheelchair. I'm so sorry Max couldn't come tonight, Ava."

"I am, too," she said, mustering a smile. "Unfortunately, one of the other pilots called out sick at the last minute, so he had to fill in."

"Well, no worries. We hired an amazing videographer, so he'll get to see the show when he gets back in town."

"Thanks, Nicholas. I'm sure he'll appreciate that."

"Darling, I'll be right back. Try to relax, okay?" He kissed the only spot on Tessa's face not blocked by the roses and headed out the door.

"These are beautiful, Ava," she said, inhaling deeply, "thank you again."

"You're welcome, and I wanted you to have them now. You should be celebrating all night. Not just after the show. Nicholas isn't the only one who's proud of you. I am, too."

Tessa carefully placed the flowers on a side table and hugged her sister. All these years she'd waited for Ava to say those words. Her oldest sister, the woman she idolized, the woman she could never live up to, the woman she loved so deeply ... *she* was proud of *her*. Whatever else happened that night, Ava's words would be a highlight of her evening.

"Hey, can I get in on this love fest? I hope you don't mind, but Nicholas told me where you all were hiding."

"I'm glad you're here." Tessa moved over to let Holly in to their now group hug.

"I feel like rock stars," she said, as they broke apart slightly but still had their arms wrapped around each other's shoulders.

"What are you talking about, Hol?"

"You know, like in all those concert documentaries we used to watch. The band always had a group huddle before they went on stage. Then someone said something inspirational, they thanked God, ran on stage, and rocked the house. Go ahead, Ava. You've always been good with that sort of thing. Plus, you're sort of our leader."

"Except, we're not all going out on stage," Ava reminded them.

"Thank goodness," Tessa snickered.

"Hey, Tessa." A woman wearing a headpiece popped her head into the doorway. "Sorry to interrupt."

"No problem, Kay, what's up."

"I just wanted to let you know, everything is good to go. Oh, and the crew wanted me to tell you to break a—"

Tessa broke out into a loud fake coughing fit to stop her before she could finish her sentence. Looking confused, and rightly so, Kay shook her head and walked off.

"You okay?" Holly asked. "There are some bottles of water over there if you need it."

"No, no," Tessa said, giving one last robust cough for good measure. "I'm just fine. The theater is so dusty." She spread her arms back out so they could get back into their group hug. "So something inspirational, right? I'll go. Since this is sort of my gig. Thank you, to my fabulous sisters, for your unending support. I know I've asked a lot of favors from you both over the years."

"A lot," Holly said under a muffled cough, jumping to the side just as Tessa threw her elbow out toward her ribcage. "You're right. It is dusty in here," she teased.

"Mmm hmm," Tessa responded. "I know I probably don't tell you both enough how much I love, admire, and appreciate you, but I do. I wouldn't be here tonight, if it weren't for you both."

"Don't sell yourself short," Ava said.

"Yeah," Holly agreed. "As much as we'd love to take the credit here, you worked your ass off."

"Mommy!"

"Sophie," Tessa exclaimed happily, breaking away from the huddle. "What are you doing back here? Where are Grandma and Grandpa?"

"They're still sitting out there with Jenna, Logan, and Ryan," Sophie replied. "Nicholas said I could come back here to see you. I wanted to say good luck."

"Thank you, sweetie." Tessa knelt down to give her daughter a hug.

"You know, Sophie," Holly told her, "in the theater, it's bad luck to say *good luck*. You're supposed to say *break a leg.*"

Ava and Tessa looked at each other with wide eyes and cracked up laughing.

"Did I miss something?" Holly asked.

"No," Tessa said. "But thank you. I'll take whatever well wishes I can get."

Peeking his head back in the door, Nicholas called into the room, "We're ready, everyone. Time to head to your seats."

36 TESSA

Tessa beamed as she stepped into the lounge, now filled with vases of roses and a bottle of champagne. The cast and crew, high on adrenaline, crowded around her—barely giving her room to breathe as they waited for her to speak.

"You all were amazing!" Tessa said, popping the bottle open and purposely spraying the contents over those who had helped make the night a huge success. "I knew you would be spectacular, but what I witnessed out there tonight was … I don't even know. What do you call something that's better than spectacular?"

"Supercalifragilisticexpialidocious?" Sophie asked, coming into the room on Nicholas' shoulders.

"Yes," Tessa laughed. "That's exactly what tonight's performance was. It was super ... um, cali – fragil—"

"... isticexpialidocious," Sophie said, finishing. "Mommy, can Logan, Jenna, Ryan, and I go collect all the flowers that were thrown on the stage?"

"Yes," Tessa replied, "thank you."

"Anyway," she continued, watching her daughter leave the room, "I would like to extend my extreme gratitude to all of you. For as hard as I've worked, I know you've all worked ten times harder. That's why my amazing husband arranged for us to have our cast party at Rocco's tonight. We've got the entire place to ourselves. You all can head over, they're expecting us with as much pizza and beer as you want."

The cast and crew cheered as they high-fived and headed toward the door.

"But not too much on the beer side!" Tessa yelled over the roar of the crowd. "We've got another show tomorrow night, folks! Do you hear me? Hello?"

It was a pointless endeavor. By the time she finished talking, she was alone in the room with Nicholas.

"We're going to have to go over there to babysit them, you know," she murmured, wrapping her arms around his neck.

"I think they'll be okay for a little bit," he said. "Besides, I kind of like having you here all to myself."

"I do, too. But where is the rest of my family?" she asked, looking around.

"Your parents and Ava are with the kids on the stage, and Holly's with Ben still out in the audience. I asked them to give us a few minutes to ourselves. I have something I need to talk to you about."

"Okay," she said. "You sound serious. It's not bad news, is it? This night is too amazing to muddle it up with bad news."

"No, my love, it's just the opposite."

Nicholas pulled a document out of his pocket and handed it to Tessa. After studying it for a moment, she looked at her husband with a huge smile across her lips.

"Is this what I think it is? How? When?"

"Remember when I followed Scott out to the parking lot last time he was here?" Nicholas asked.

"Yes," Tessa said. "Yes, you said you went out there to give him a piece of your mind, and that you decided not to prosecute, out of respect for Sophie."

"That's right. When I first told him I knew what he did with the money, he denied it, of course," Nicholas explained. "Then I showed him the pictures and the receipt for the television … and I mentioned that I'd spoken with his boss. The same boss he's had all these years."

"You didn't tell me that part. I wish I could have been there to see the expression on his face. I miss all of the fun!"

"It was pretty fun. Especially when he started blubbering. Right there in the parking lot, and admitted everything, begging me to forgive him. I have to tell you, Tess. He's not an attractive man when his eyes and mouth scrunch all together. I really think you made a better choice with me."

"For so many reasons," she replied, laughing. "So what did he say exactly?"

"Well, that he only contacted you because he saw that you'd come into money. Then I asked him if he'd ever had any intention of being Sophie's father."

"And?" she asked, raising her brows.

"He said he didn't even know you'd had a girl until he saw her in the wedding picture."

Tessa nodded. All these years and he'd never even cared enough to find out. "So I'm guessing you told him that if he signed the papers you wouldn't prosecute."

"No. It was never my intention to prosecute, and I didn't want him to think I was blackmailing him. I was going to suggest he pay the money back directly to Sophie into a trust account we set up on her behalf. However, before I could get two words out, he said he was in no position to support her, and he could see she was happy having me around. He then said he wanted for me to adopt her, and was willing to relinquish all legal rights."

"Just like that?"

"I was skeptical as well," Nicholas said. "So I told him I'd have my lawyers draw up the papers and overnight them to him. He had them signed, notarized, and returned to me within the week."

"And you never discussed prosecution?" Tessa asked.

"That's the crazy part," Nicholas said. "We never actually did."

"So if he tries to contact Sophie again, we have that in our back pocket."

"Exactly," Nicholas said, "but I wouldn't worry about him coming back again. He knows the evidence against him is stacked pretty high. Once the adoption goes through, I'd really like to just forget Scott Warren ever existed. I was dying to tell you, but I didn't want to distract you until after opening night. My lawyer is drawing up the official adoption papers as we speak. That is, if it's okay with you and Sophie."

"Are you kidding?" she asked, jumping into Nicholas' arms. "Of course it's okay. It's what I've wanted all along, and I happen to know for a fact that Sophie will be thrilled."

"About what?" Sophie asked, coming into the room with an armful of flowers in every color possible. "Mommy, aren't they beautiful? Do we get to keep them?"

"Well," Tessa said, pulling out a pink daisy, tearing off most of the stem, and tucking it behind her daughter's ear, "we have to share them with everyone who worked on the play. But, you and Jenna, and the boys if they want, can pick out a few to keep."

"Okay. They're still collecting flowers on the stage. Aunt Ava said we weren't allowed to come back here yet, but I snuck away to show you these. I'm not in trouble, am I?"

"Of course not, honey." Taking the flowers from her daughter and putting them on the floor, Tessa knelt down with Nicholas next to her. "Actually, Nicholas and I need to talk to you. Do you remember what you said to me a while back ... the last time Scott was here, right after he left? The part about who you wished your father was?"

Sophie looked a Nicholas and smiled before looking down at her fidgeting feet.

"It's okay, honey. You don't have to be embarrassed," Tessa said, taking her hand. "We just want to be sure it's what you really want."

"You mean it can happen?" she asked, sounding confused. "You can make Nicholas be my real daddy?"

"If that's what you want, then yes, we can," she said, looking to her husband. "Is it?"

"Oh, yes!" she cried, throwing her arms around Nicholas' neck. "That's exactly what I want."

Nicholas stood up and swung her around. "It's exactly what I want, too, Sophie."

Tessa wrapped her arms around her family. "It's what I want as well. In fact, I think it's the most supercalifragilisticexpialidocious idea ever!"

"Daddy?" Sophie asked, looking up at Nicholas.

"Yes, daughter?" he replied, his voice full of love and compassion.

"Do you think we can still get a puppy?" she asked sweetly.

Yup, wrapped right around her little finger, Tessa thought as she hugged her family even tighter.

37 HOLLY

"**S**ounds like a party in here." Holly entered the room with Ava, her parents, and the rest of the children behind her, all carrying armfuls of flowers. "Is it okay to come in now? Sophie! We were looking for you!"

"Yes, come in, come in," Nicholas said, waving everybody into the room. "Sophie's fine, we were just talking."

"Tessa," Holly began, "I know you're probably getting tired of hearing this, but the show was incredible."

"Nope, not sick of it at all," she replied, grinning. "Thank you. In fact, feel free to say it as many times as you'd like for the rest of my life. Hey, where's Ben? You didn't leave the poor guy sitting all by himself in the empty audience did you?"

"Nah," Holly said. "He's making his way down the hall in his wheelchair. I offered to help, but you know how stubborn he can be. Mr. Independent is determined to get here all by himself. He'll show up eventually."

"The play was fabulous, honey," Tessa's mom said, giving her a huge hug and kiss on the cheek.

Her father and Ava followed suit with similar compliments and accolades.

"Guess what?" Sophie said, the smile on her face stretching from ear to ear.

"What, sweetheart?" Ava asked.

"Nicholas is going to be my daddy. *My real daddy.*"

"Is he?" Holly asked, looking to Tessa for answers.

She held up the paper, even though there was no way they would be able to read it from where they stood. "Scott agreed it would be best for Sophie if Nicholas were her father," Tessa explained, talking particularly slow, presumably in an attempt to let her family know she was choosing her words carefully while speaking in front of her daughter, "so Nicholas is officially adopting her. It's all going to be legal very soon. I just found out myself." Putting her arm around Nicholas' waist, Tessa glowed. "My amazing husband surprised us with the paperwork just now. As you can see, Sophie is thrilled. We all are."

"Oh, honey," Ava said. "That's wonderful news. Congratulations. To all of you."

"It's about time. I never did like that bast—" Tessa's father started, but stopped when his wife swiftly covered his mouth with her hand.

"We couldn't be happier for you," she said, glowing.

Their dad vigorously nodded, hand still securely in place.

"Absolutely! We're so happy for you," Holly agreed, hugging each of them. She knew there had to be some amazing story behind it all, but she was practically bursting at the seams to show off her own surprise. There would be plenty of time to hear the Scott saga as they celebrated later once the children went home with her parents. Right now she had her own good news to share. "This night is turning into quite an evening, don't you think? It's just one surprise after another after another."

"There's more?" Ava asked.

"Well, now that you mention it …" Holly burst out into her own huge smile and said, "Wait here," before running out of the room. Moments later, she returned, with Max behind her.

"Max!" Ava yelled, running up to her husband. "What are you doing here? I thought you said you had to work tonight."

"I found a replacement" he replied, hugging his wife and children. "I snuck in during the first act and sat in the back. I didn't want to cause a scene since I wasn't expected. Get it? *Scene?"* He waited for non-existent laughter to end and then continued. "Amazing work, Tessa. Really great."

"Thanks, Max," Tessa said. "I'm really glad you could make it."

"There's no way I could stay away and miss your show. Besides the fact that you'd never let me live it down," he said, "we're family, and there's nothing more important. Anyway, the party's just getting started," he added, sneaking a glance at Holly.

"Hey, did someone say something about a party?"

Max stepped to the side as all eyes turned to Ben, *standing* in the doorway.

"Oh my God! Ben! You're walking," Tessa screamed, running over to him.

"Well, it's more like pushing and dragging," he said, gripping his walker with white knuckles.

"I can't believe you kept this a secret, Holly," Ava said. "This is amazing. When did this start?"

"Earlier in the week," she said, proudly. "Ben took his first step on Monday. Once he got going, there was no stopping him either. He's been walking up and down the halls of the rehab center nonstop. His parents have been here with him the last few days. They told me to tell you they're sorry they couldn't stay for the show, but Ben's father had a business dinner he couldn't miss," Holly said looking at Tessa. "Anyway, the therapist finally took his walker away to make him rest. He didn't want him overdoing it the first week. He only gave it back to him for tonight so he could show you all, but Ben promised to take it easy and spend most of the night in his wheelchair."

"Yeah, like that's gonna happen," he said with a smirk. They watched cautiously as he moved one leg at a time, making his way into the room at a snail's pace. "Slow and steady wins the race, isn't that what they say?"

"You're doing great, babe," Holly said, with the same amount of pride and encouragement she'd carried throughout each of his tedious therapy sessions. "By the time you start pushing the stroller, you'll be a pro."

"Stroller?" Ava asked. "Is that part of therapy?"

"No," Holly replied, a huge smile crossing her lips. "That's part of parenthood. We're expecting!"

"But how?" Ava said. "I thought you didn't want to do IVF again."

"Well," Ben began, "when a man and a woman love each other—"

"Stop." Shaking her hand, Ava put her hand up. "I know *how*. And don't forget there are children in the room. I just thought …"

"It happened naturally. Before the accident, when we stopped trying. Go figure," Holly said, laughing. "We're just as surprised as anyone. And it looks like we made it past the first trimester this time. I'm not surprised. If this little peanut could survive all of the stress I've been under so far, she …"

"... or he," Ben added as he shuffled his feet.

"Or he, is a real fighter. Just like his or her daddy."

"Wow, Holly! First the news about Ben and now this! I'm so incredibly happy for you," Tessa said, hugging her. "For both of you!"

"You have no idea how hard it was to keep my mouth shut about all of this. I was going crazy. Ben's parents were the only ones who knew. They didn't tell you, did they?" she asked, looking at her parents.

"No," her mom replied, looking stunned with tears rolling down her face. "We're so surprised. In a good way, of course."

"Indeed," her father added as they all embraced. "A very, very good way."

"Amazing news, truly," Nicholas said, getting in line to hug Holly next. "And, Ben, I never doubted for a moment you'd be out of that chair. In fact, this time next year, I expect to see you running marathons."

"I don't know about that," Ben replied, "but I do know we really have you to thank. I can't imagine being up and around like this without the team you brought in. Holly and I are truly forever indebted."

"Nonsense. We're family," he replied. "It's like Max said. There's nothing more important. We do whatever we can to help each other."

"This is all so fantastic," Ava said, waiting patiently for her turn to hug her sister and brother-in-law. "I really think I'm in shock."

38 AVA

"Are you okay?" Holly asked as Ava stepped back.

"Yes. It's just ... this is all so unbelievable," she said, looking around the room. "A star studded night for Tessa, a new daddy for Sophie, Ben's walking and going to be a parent along with you, and Max is here. This night is incredible."

"It's not over yet," Max said, taking Ava's hands. "There's another surprise."

She noticed that her sisters were surrounding her now with the goofiest smiles on their faces. In fact everyone in the room, except for the kids, who were back to flower sorting in the corner, had weird expressions.

"What's going on here?" she asked. "This isn't one of those crazy interventions or something, is it?"

"Actually, it kind of is," Max told her.

"Okay, you guys are making me a little nervous. Can we just go back to celebrating everyone else's good news? And Tessa. Let's not forget this is her big night! Can't whatever this *thing* is wait? I promise I won't skip town or anything."

"Av," Tessa said, "you don't understand. What Max is about to tell you is part of the celebration. I *wanted* him to tell you tonight. You deserve this after everything you've done for me. It's what I was trying to tell you before. You give to Holly and me and the kids and Max not stop, but especially to me, I think. So, it's an honor to share my celebration with you. What Max is about to tell you … well, it's just the most amazing thing. You're just not going to believe—"

"Um, Tessa?" Ben finally said after several unsuccessful throat clears.

She looked at him and started laughing. "I'm doing that thing, aren't I? Where someone has big news, and I keep talking and talking and almost spoil the surprise?"

"Yes," Max and Ben both answered together.

"Okay, fine," she muttered, backing away. "Go ahead, Max."

"Thanks," he said, bringing his attention back to his wife. "Tessa's right you know. You give so much to everyone else. And in the process, you've given up so much."

"No," Ava said, "we already talked about this. It's what we agreed to."

"I know we talked about it, but—"

"It's what was best for the kids."

"Ava Haines Wallis!" Holly exclaimed, taking a step in. "Will you stop interrupting and just listen to your husband?"

"Fine," she said, rolling her eyes at her. "I'm sorry, Max. I don't want you to think I regret anything, because I really don't."

"I know that, Ava. I also know that when I took you to the gallery, there was a sparkle in your eyes I hadn't seen in years. A sparkle I greatly miss."

Yes, there was no denying that being surrounded by art again brought out a passion she'd tucked away years ago. But it didn't mean anything. She could easily tuck it back away anytime she wanted.

"So I enjoyed our date," she said, her defenses getting the best of her. "It just means we need to go on more of them."

"That I agree with," he said, smiling. "Do you remember during our date when Jenna called you, and you stepped outside to take the call?"

"Yes," she replied, tilting her head. Just what did that have to do with anything?

"Well, Gene, the owner of the gallery, began talking to me. Gushing is more like it. It seems he thinks you've got quite an eye for gallery work."

"Oh," she waved him off in a dismissive manner, "I just made a few simple suggestions when I stopped by on my own one day. It was no big deal."

"I don't know about that," Max said. "He asked me if you were looking for part-time work ... said he could really use someone like you around."

"Well, I'm sure he was just being nice," she said. "Besides, I have the kids to look after. I wouldn't be able to work there."

"That's what I told him," he said.

"What?" It was one thing for her to turn a job offer down, but for Max to tell him no? He had no right! Hurt and anger began to set in.

"Well, I told him that if he asked you directly, you'd say you couldn't take the job because of the kids. However, I told him not to worry, that we'd find a way to make it work. After all, Jenna and Logan are in school all day, and Ryan can go with Mrs. Connelly three days a week. I hope you don't mind—I already asked her. Congratulations, Ava. You're officially back in business. If you want the job that is."

"Are you serious?"

"Completely," he responded. "This is what you want, isn't it?"

"Yes! I just had no idea. I was only on the phone for a few minutes," she laughed, giving him a hug. "Thank you for doing this for me."

"I really didn't do anything," he said. "I just want to see you happy. There is a slight problem, though."

Sighing, she hung her head down. Why did there always have to be a problem? "What is it?" she asked, afraid of the answer.

"Gene doesn't want you to start right away."

"Um, okay," Ava said. It was an odd request, but he was the boss. "Did he say why?"

"Well, he said he wants to wait until you get back from Paris," Max said, a coy smile slowly appearing.

"From … Paris?" She turned to her sister. "Did he just say Paris?"

Holly nodded.

"But—" she started.

"Yes, Ava, Paris," Max interjected. "Don't you remember? When I proposed to you? I promised that one day, I would fly you to Paris so we could visit your favorite art museum, the Musée de l'Orangerie, to see Monet's *Water Lilies* in person. I know how much you adore them. Well, I had hoped it wouldn't take me twelve years to make it happen, but you know what they say, better late than never."

"But the kids …"

"Are staying with us." Tessa jokingly shook her finger at her sister. "And if you start another sentence with *but,* I'm going to kick your butt. You're going, Ava, whether you want to or not."

"I want to!" she squealed, throwing her arms around Max. "I want to!"

As Ava stepped back and glanced around the room, she noticed that for the first time in a very long time, every person had a smile on their face.

"I told you this was going to be a great night," Holly said, taking Ava's hands.

"The best," Tessa added, breaking in to form a circle of three.

"No," Ava told them, "the best is yet to come. For all of us."

EXCERPT: MERRY WISHES ~ A WHISPERED WISHES EBOOK NOVELLA

"Were you surprised?" Ava asked.

Carly sat on one of the boxes in what would eventually be her living room. She knew she should be unpacking, but at the moment, even the simplest task seemed overwhelming. She'd much rather chat with her old college friend over the telephone. They hadn't seen each other in what felt like forever, but when they talked it seemed as if only days had gone by since they'd last been together. It was the mark of all good friends. "You knew about it?" she asked.

"Of course I knew about it. Parker called me. I was even planning on being there, but Jenna got sick, and Max had to work. She didn't tell you?"

"No. She must have forgotten. Now that would have been some surprise. It's been ages since we've seen each other. Too long."

"Agreed. Let's make plans after the holidays. So, how've you been holding up? You've been on my mind a lot lately."

"I don't know," Carly told her. "I have good days and bad days. I'm glad to be done with that idiot, but at the same time, I can't believe the life we built together is gone. All those years together—poof— vanished into thin air like they never even existed ... like *I never even existed*. Some days I want to strangle him. Scratch that. Most days I want to strangle him."

"Personally, I think you're showing remarkable restraint. And strangle isn't exactly the word that comes to mind in your situation," Ava said.

"That sounds like something I would say. After all this time, have I finally worn off on you?"

"I'm just looking out for you. The same way you've always looked out for me. The Carly I know is a no nonsense go-getter with a heart of gold. That jerk took advantage of your heart. It's only natural you'd be feeling the way you're feeling. Take some time to heal. Find what makes you happy."

"Friends like you make me happy ... and painting. Oh! Did I tell you I've been commissioned for a big job? A designer wants my work for her fabrics. This could be my big break. Wouldn't that be something?" She jumped up, excited to be telling her good friend about her news. They'd been art students together at Wolfenson. If anyone would be thrilled for her, it would be Ava.

"Well, I'm not surprised. You're amazing. I'm so excited for you!"

"I'm pretty excited, too. I should start unpacking, though. I need to find a spot in this mess to set up shop until I have a real studio. The great Marilyn Keyes has me on a tight deadline."

"Marilyn Keyes? You forgot to mention that part! That's huge, Carly. Okay, I'm going to hang up now. You need to get to work. Have I told you I'm proud of you?"

"No, but thanks, I appreciate it. Love you, Ava. I'll talk to you soon."

"Love you, too."

Carly hung up the phone and let out a long, deep breath while looking at the unending piles of boxes. "Focus," she whispered to herself. "You can do this." Walking to the far corner of the room toward the set of windows that overlooked her expansive gardens, she began to carve out a space she could potentially be comfortable in ... temporarily at least. She slid furniture and other large pieces out of the way, as she imagined the placement of her easel and other painting supplies that would eventually wind up there. For the moment, those items were tucked away amongst all of her boxes and other random items. She hadn't been the most organized in her packing efforts.

Smiling, Carly looked forward to the day when she'd finally have a real art studio. She could have chosen to use the spare bedroom on the second floor of her home, but wanted use of a larger space and instead chose the unfinished attic that made up the third floor. That way, she could have more control over the direction of the incoming light. *That must be it.* She had a vague recollection of labeling all of the boxes that held items for her studio "third floor." The movers probably put everything in the attic. As she began to climb the stairs, she heard a knock.

"Crap," she muttered, turning back around. *I really don't have time to play meet the neighbors right now.* "Who is it?"

"Anthony Conly. Here to give you an estimate. You did say two o'clock, didn't you?"

"Right," she lied and made her way over to the door, swinging it open. She'd completely forgotten he was coming by today, but he was the one person she actually did have time for. "Yes, hello, come in." An older man, with thinning hair and weathered skin who reminded her of her father, stood in her doorway. "I'm Carly Cater. Thanks for stopping by. The room I want to renovate is on the third floor. Follow me." She started up the stairs for the second time with Anthony behind her.

An hour later, after taking measurements and discussing specs, Anthony presented her with an estimate, which appeared to be reasonable. Not that she would know the difference, but it was within the amount of cash she had on hand to get the job done. He also helped her move several boxes she found with her painting supplies down to the first floor. All in all, it was turning out to be a productive afternoon.

"I'd like to get started right away," Carly said as she walked him out to his van. "What kind of time frame are we looking at?"

"Well, I'll need to make a few phone calls to set up a crew, and we'll need permits for some of the work, but at the very least, we should be able to do some basic framing starting next week, if you want."

A wide smile crossed her face. "Yes, I want."

"Great. I'll need to get a deposit from you for materials and to pay my guys. If that's agreeable, then I'll see you next Monday at seven a.m."

"That's no problem. Thank you so much, Anthony," she said, holding out her hand for a shake. "It's been a pleasure meeting you."

About the Author

Karen Pokras writes adult contemporary and middle grade fiction under the names Karen Pokras and Karen Pokras Toz. Her books have won several awards including two Readers' Favorite Book Awards, the Grand Prize in the Purple Dragonfly Book Awards, as well as placing first for two Global E-Book Awards for Pre-Teen Literature. A native of Connecticut, Karen now lives outside of Philadelphia with her family. For more information, visit www.karenpokras.com and www.karentoz.com

It's hard to believe I'm saying good-bye to the Haines sisters. They've been a part of my writing life for so long now, they feel like family. As always, there are many gracious folks who helped bring this book and entire series to life. First, to my family and friends, thank you for your everlasting love and support. I'm truly a lucky lady to have you all in my life. To my beta readers, Kathie and Megan, thank you for your thoughtful comments and critical eye. You have no idea how helpful you both are to me! To my editor, Melissa Ringsted, *See what happened was …* I'll never be able to write those words in another book again without laughing! Thanks for not only being a great editor, but also for being a great friend. To my amazing cover designer and team at Najla Qamber Designs, you all are incredibly talented. I loved working with you! And to Author A.B. Shepherd — once again, thank you for naming my series! You're the best!

And to my readers—you're the reason I do this, so thank you for believing in me and for your overwhelming support. Feel free to drop me a line - **I love hearing from you!**

karenpokrasauthor@gmail.com

Whispered Wishes Series:
Book 1: Ava's Wishes
Book 2: Holly's Wishes
Book 3: Tessa's Wishes
Book 4: Woven Wishes
Merry Wishes: A Whispered Wishes Novella

Chasing Invisible (Karen Pokras Toz)

Books for Children 7-12 (Karen Pokras Toz)
Nate Rocks the World
Nate Rocks the Boat
Nate Rocks the School
Nate Rocks the City
Millicent Marie Is Not My Name
Pie and Other Brilliant Idea